THE MOSQUITO TEST

by

Richard Kent

A Windswept Book
Windswept House Publishers
Mt. Desert, Maine 04660

ISBN 1-883650-03-8
Library of Congress Catalogue No. 93-061634

Printed in the United States of America

The author has donated his profits from the sale of this book to the Cystic Fibrosis Foundation and to the Jimmy Fund of the Dana Farber Cancer Institute.

Acknowledgments

Special thanks to Nancy Dorr, Paula Dupill, Erica Violette, and Monica Wood for helping with this novel.

Also thanks to my student colleagues for patiently listening to various parts of the book.

Sincere appreciation to Anne Wood for her guidance, her expertise, and her friendship.

This book was inspired by Barbara, Dorothy, Leon, and Carla
as well as Erica, Neil, Peggy, Stephanie, Danielle, and Tom,
for their battles well fought.

*

And is dedicated to
Allen, my hero.

The bottom line was numbers.

Percentages.

Odds.

The doctor said, "Better than seventy percent success rate." Seventy percent, I thought. Three out of ten die. 30 out of 100. 300 out of 1000. I hated those numbers — they turned my stomach, scared me senseless. Every time I went through them, the odds seemed worse.

Then there were those books. Everyone had a book I should read; I must have received eight or ten that first month alone. They all told the same sort of cancer story. I wanted to shove the things down their throats. I hardly ever read while I was healthy, so the last thing I wanted to do was read about some terminally ill thirteen-year-old in Bloomington, Indiana, who lived his last two years inspiring all those around him with his courage and zest for life. It was plain old crap. Dead is dead.

* * *

The players and Coach Kiesman had asked me to sit on the bench for the season — they'd even given me a uniform to wear. But I couldn't. It just didn't seem right.

I knew I would have made the team; there was no question about that. Everyone knew. I would have been the first sophomore in six years to make the varsity basketball squad at St. John's High School. Danny Rouleau did it as a tenth grader and he went on to star at the University of Maine. What a jump shot. Incredible.

But I couldn't even try out. Doctor's orders, "No contact sports." So there was no way I was going to suit up and sit on the bench of a team I hadn't made.

Instead, I sat up in the "Ozone" with my friends to watch the first game of the season. Only certain kids could sit up in the top row of the bleachers and chant cheers against the referees and the players from the other teams. Only certain kids could sit in the "Ozone" wearing Hawaiian shirts and Bermuda shorts in the dead of a Maine winter.

I didn't dress up or cheer. I guess I was feeling sorry for myself because I wanted to be out on the floor playing point guard, not sitting in the bleachers screaming stupid-ass cheers. But there was nothing I could do, and at least in the "Ozone" I felt the game.

"TIME FOR A CHECK-UP REF!" screamed Kevin as he held up a huge eye chart. "Frigging guy is blind," he raved, sitting back down as I patted him on the shoulder. "My frig — ging grandmother could have seen that one." His voice slipped up an octave as he stood back up waving the chart. Kevin Beane was my best friend. When I was diagnosed, a lot of kids just sort of disappeared, and a lot of them wouldn't do anything with me unless someone else was along. As if I were going to drop dead walking through the mall or driving to McDonald's. I understood in a way. It didn't make me feel any better, but I did understand.

When I was in elementary school, I had known a kid who got cancer. His face swelled up and he waddled as he walked. One day he just never came back to school. Our teacher told us that Lincoln had gone to some kind of special hospital that would help him. He died the next summer.

Lincoln had scared me, too. I never knew what to say to him. It's weird. What the hell do you say to a kid with cancer? "How's life?" But that's just what Kevin always asked. He had a kind of sense of what was right — he rarely went too far one way or the other. He made me feel comfortable. He made me feel normal.

Some kids were tough to be around. They made me feel really sick as if the cancer was crawling all over my skin for everyone to see. And some of the cheerleaders killed me. They turned on the old tears like their phony rah-rah smiles and always ended up running out of the room weeping as if it were their insides rotting out. It always turned out this way — somehow they got pitied. Somehow they were the injured party. Incredible.

Then, the teachers. Some were really cool and knew exactly how to act and what to say. Others hid. A few didn't seem to care. And then the ones who spit out so much philosophical bull about life that it was like watching those screaming, slick-haired preachers on Sunday morning television. They were the ones I stayed away from — they just didn't understand. It's easy to spit out quotes about life when your life is okay.

That night we blew away the Hall School 78 to 45, and the guys in the "Ozone" made a scene just like always. It got so bad at one point that a couple of the teachers had to come up and calm things down. We'd hear about that on the intercom come Monday morning, that's for sure.

I had always liked watching what happened at the final buzzer of a game. How'd the losing coach take it — what did the players do. But after this game there were no handshakes. Coach Kiesman and the two captains shot right to the scorer's table and the microphone.

"Would you all please stay in your seats," said the coach.

Everyone sat. People listened when Coach spoke.

All the players from both teams lined up on either side of him as if there had been no game, as if the thing were just about to start. It had been well rehearsed.

A chill shot up my spine.

"We'd like to dedicate this game . . ." his voice echoed over the speakers through the gym, ". . . to a young man — one of our teammates — who's waging his own battle, one we know he'll win. Scott Cinader."

The crowd stood. Coach Kiesman held the game ball high above his head. Everyone turned toward me. They all knew where the kid with cancer was sitting.

I moved slowly from the top of the bleachers past all the kids in the Ozone. My whole body quivered and my scalp tingled with beads of sweat. At that moment I had no clear thoughts and couldn't focus on anything or anyone. I just walked, staring at the red steps of the wooden bleachers.

Once I crossed the court, I felt the ball being wedged into my arms. My hair was ruffled. My back slapped. My butt patted. Then, everyone disappeared.

The teams jogged into their locker rooms. The crowd filed by, but not too close. And the next thing I heard was Kevin whispering into my ear as he guided me out of the gymnasium.

My mother was waiting up for me in the kitchen when I got home. She had always stayed up until I got home when I was healthy. She'd lie in bed reading and call out "Good night" as I tip-toed past her room. But now, she stood guard in the kitchen — I knew it just made her feel better to see me face to face. "How was the game?" she asked looking me over, making sure there were no signs of fatigue.

"We won 78-45."

She ignored the score and eyed the ball. "What do you have that for?" A tinge of suspicion sounded in her voice as if she expected me to admit that I'd played in the game.

"It's the game ball," I whispered. "They gave it to me."

"They presented you with the game ball?" She took the ball and held it gently, turning it over and over in her hands. "What a wonderful thing. Beautiful. Oh, I wish I had been there. Your father will be so thrilled." Tears coated her eyes, but she would not cry.

That was my mother. I could feel her strength, and I felt healthier when I was near her. She knew we all had to get on with it. One day at a time. One hour at a time. Moment to moment. Everyone always talked about how strong my mother was — how she kept the doctors and the nurses in line — how she knew more about my disease than almost anyone. Most of all she knew how to keep my father and me from dwelling on it.

She never used to be that way. She always cried at sad, old movies, and whenever I was presented an athletic award, she could barely see through the camera lens for the great flood of tears. My disease changed her.

"Time for bed, don't you think?" she said, placing the ball on the kitchen counter. "May I keep this to show Dad? He'll be back a little later."

"Sure."

As I headed out of the door, my mother said, "Don't forget, we have a treatment tomorrow."

We. I knew she didn't mean anything by it, but sometimes she could say stuff that would really tick me off. Like maybe she was going to have a dose of the chemo juice. Like maybe she'd like to try her hand at vomiting until her throat was bleeding and her stomach was ripping apart.

Don't forget. And how the hell do you forget something like chemotherapy?

"10 A.M."

"Yes, Ma. 10 A.M. Tomorrow. At the medical center, right? The outpatient clinic, right?" I knew I'd overdone it.

"Sorry. Sometimes I forget you're not my little boy anymore." She didn't say it as if she wanted any kind of pity; she was matter-of-fact, straightforward. She knew.

I nodded and put on my tough-guy face, but as I walked up to my bedroom I felt like a little boy again. Frightened. Alone. I wanted to sit in her lap and watch television. I wanted to listen to her read. And sometimes at night since I'd gotten ill, I wanted to crawl into my parents' bed, right between them both, to snuggle up where it was warm and safe. Sometimes, I was scared to death.

The sheets of my bed were cold as I pulled them up to my chin and then over my head. Soon, the same thoughts. I folded the sheets back down to my chin and propped my head up on the pillow.

Soft sheets. Satin white. My head raised as if I were in my own coffin wearing the same dark blue suit that my mother had picked out for my cousin's wedding. I lay dead still, hands crossed, like my grandfather in his coffin.

I pictured my funeral and my friends filing by. Felt the power I had over them. I showed them. I was dead. They'd never get to see me again.

They cried and their eyes glanced toward me but then quickly beyond.

Look at me!

But they kept on walking.

Out of sight. Away.

Gone forever. Then, as always, the cover of the coffin began to close. I felt as if I had jumped off a tall building with nothing but concrete below. My insides tried to bust out. I wanted to scream, but it wouldn't come, like I was drowning, like there was no air at all.

It always ended the same way.

It always ended in the dark. Dead is dead.

— 2 —

My mother wouldn't allow herself to play tennis after I'd been diagnosed. At first there just wasn't enough time with all the doctors' appointments and the barrage of tests. Then, if she wasn't in the hospital, she was at the insurance agency, and if she wasn't at the blood bank, she was at the drug store. Even after things had settled down, when the chemotherapy sessions had become routine, when her daily jaunts to one place or another on my behalf could be knocked off in a couple of hours, she just couldn't think about it.

A tennis game.

She told me later that she used to sit and watch me take the chemo juice, then hold the little plastic pan as I vomited, and all the while her only clear thoughts were of the rhythm of her serve and of the careful, level swing of her backhand. At the time, those thoughts were her salvation. Her escape. But she said she always ended up feeling guilty. Her son's life was in jeopardy, and she was dreaming about a ball and a racket . . . a silly game.

I finally coaxed her back to the tennis courts the same way I got most everything when I was a kid — I badgered her. I bugged her, and I loved it, that is until she came back from her first day at the courts with "the plan."

My mother always had plans. The thing is they inevitably included my father and me. We'd end up modeling some crazy outfit at a spring fashion show to raise money for snow leopards or judging apple pie contests at the church. Sampling pies was great, but picking a winner while facing the cooks — 20 or so grandmothers whose lives revolved around cooking and making people happy — gave me nightmares.

That was my mother, if it wasn't a plan, it was a cause. And this day, I was both.

"I called Dr. Schmidt this evening."

"You did. Why?"

"I wanted to see what he thought about your playing tennis."

"Tennis?" It was as if she had served swordfish and broccoli.

"Yes. Tennis," she said trying to hide her reaction. "He thought it was a great idea."

"Tennis."

At first I was sure she was kidding. I didn't do tennis. Neither did any of my friends. We played soccer, basketball, and lacrosse — those were the sports that jocks played at St. John's. Tennis was something my mother and the other ladies played so they could gab and then not feel guilty for having a lot to eat at the Club. She wasn't kidding.

"You could come down to The Racket and take lessons."

"With all those old ladies?"

"Old?"

"You know what I mean."

"Yes, I do. Anyway, they have a youth program."

"Yeah, a bunch of ten-year-old yard apes who'll smoke my butt."

"Everybody has to start somewhere."

I didn't answer hoping she would figure out that I wasn't interested in starting tennis anywhere at any time. No such luck. She was not one to give in easily.

"A little frightened?"

"You kidding? I just . . ." But before I could come up with the right words, she closed the door.

"Good. I'll pick you up after school tomorrow for your first class."

And that was it — she got me. The same way I usually got her. The same way my father played our family game — a quick attack, a solid challenge, no space or time for retaliation. We were good at this game, my mom and dad and I. And we rarely broke the rules, especially the most important one: when you were gotten, it was over. History. No complaints. No crying. You just paid the price and lost with dignity . . . and waited, waited for the next round to get even.

That evening at supper my father played the next round of the family game, and I was his accomplice. As always, my mom walked right into it.

"Scott's going to begin tennis lessons tomorrow," she announced.

My dad stared at her as if she were being levitated above the kitchen table. "Tennis?" (Dad didn't like swordfish and broccoli either.)

"Yes. Tennis." My mother had one of those looks on her face — kind of hurt, yet proud and unyielding.

I cupped my hands to cover my smile. My dad was incredible at keeping a straight face.

"With you and the girls?" he asked incredulously.

I dropped my head. Bit my lower lip.

"No, in the youth program. Dr. Schmidt thought it was a great idea. Getting Scott out on the courts for a little exercise would really help him."

"You want to play?" he asked, knowing I was on the edge of losing it completely.

I shrugged.

"Tennis, huh?" My father sat reflectively and rubbed his chin. He looked at me, then he looked at my mom — he was ready to score. "Well, I guess until he can play a real sport, it'll have to do."

My mom flinched, but she didn't bite. She could play the game with the best of them. And, I knew, she'd get her turn.

* * *

Most of the time I felt invisible in the hallways at school. I liked that. I could disappear in the hustle, amongst the hundreds of faces. In the hallways I was just another kid fighting for space and the fast lane to class. But sometimes, when I least expected it, when the hallways were thinning before the bell or when the droves of students clogged to a stop because of a fight or a *Playboy* centerfold hung above a doorway, I would catch someone's eye. And there it was, that look, the stare that said in an instant, "Don't get near me. I don't want to catch it."

I knew deep inside that most of those kids hated themselves for showing that flicker of fear. And sometimes I felt so bad that I wanted to say, "Hey, don't worry about it, it's no big deal." But, of course, that wasn't true.

There were days when I could go seven periods in a row without getting that look. Entire days when I didn't think about it. Days when I'd be just another kid complaining about homework assignments or checking out Cathy McNear.

Holy. Cathy McNear. A perfect 10 if there ever was one. The girl who supplied more fantasy time to the boys of St. John's than *Playboy* and *Hustler* combined. And as Kevin always said, "She could chill out a frigging popsicle!"

It had been a good day, but I was swamped with work. I threw my books down on a library table. The girl at the other end was a cheerleader; her name was Lori James. She wore perfect clothes, didn't have a hair out of place. Usually girls like her didn't sit alone in the library or any place for that matter. But looking at the stack of books in front of her, I figured she had a lot of homework to do, and no time to socialize. That was fine by me; I had to analyze Robert Frost's "Stopping by Woods on a Snowy Evening" and write a two-pager on the poem before the next period.

I pressed down the pages of my anthology and got to reading.

"Whose woods these are I think I know.

His house is in the village, though;"

Oh brother, how can anyone get into this stuff?

"He will not see me stopping here

To watch his woods fill up with snow."

Holy.

"My little horse must think it queer"

Not as queer as this poem.

"To stop without a farmhouse near

Between the woods and frozen lake La-la, la-la, ta-ta Mistake."

Roses are red, footballs are brown, I'll smash your face into the ground.

I glanced up from the poem and noticed Lori looking at me. Her eyes darted back to her work. I returned to mine.

"The only other sound's the sweep

Of easy wind and downy flake."

This sucks! Why would anyone read this stuff?

I felt the presence again, that strange feeling you get when you know someone's watching you. I glanced out of the corner of my eye. Lori was staring. Sometimes you can just tell what someone's thinking by the way they look. Like when Kevin stared at Cathy McNear — you didn't have to be Einstein to figure out what his perverted little mind was conjuring up.

When I looked at Lori, I knew instantly — the "kid-with-cancer" stare. I knew she didn't want to, but she couldn't help herself. It's like passing a car accident. You just can't help looking. You don't really want to see some guy with his head wedged through the windshield and blood smeared all over the place, but in a way you do. "That's the human beast," my father always said. And it's true. We humans can be pretty strange at times.

Finally, I stared back at her. Caught. She didn't know how to escape. Her face seemed to lose its color as she fumbled for her pen without looking down. Our eyes were locked, and I was sure that at that moment her insides screamed. But I refused to let go. For some reason I wanted her to squirm. I wanted to make her feel bad. I'd never done that to anyone before.

"Well, that's that," she said, closing her books and standing up, her eyes tearing away from mine.

She snatched her pen and was gone.

"The woods are lovely, dark, and deep, But I have promises to keep, And miles to go before I sleep, And miles to go before I sleep."

And miles to go before I sleep.

— 3 —

There were six kids milling around Court One waiting for our instructor, a woman named Barbara Allen. My mother said she was really nice and a great coach. A couple of the kids obviously knew each other and stood off to the side laughing and talking easily. But the rest of us poor slobs were strangers, and we picked at our racket strings, looked at our shoes, and avoided any kind of eye contact as we waited. I felt useless.

Only the two guys who knew each other seemed at all athletic — the rest were quite a sight. Tall and awkward. Short and fat. And one guy who looked malnourished. I couldn't believe it. Here I was: from varsity athlete to a member of the Rejects of America Club all in six weeks. And there was nothing I could do, especially since my mother had sprung for a new racket and six weeks of lessons.

Ms. Allen walked onto Court One. For an older woman like my mother, she was nice looking — blonde and very athletic. "Come on over here, guys," she called, in a soft but confident voice.

I stood back and watched my new classmates gather around her. They were quite a group, and as always, I already had them nicknamed. Dumpy waddled over as if he had a load in his pants. Stretch, a tall gooky guy, looked as if he could have tripped over one of the lines on the court. And then the skinny kid, Twig — his arms weren't any bigger than the shaft of his tennis racket. These guys were quite a sight.

Ms. Allen had us introduce ourselves. Dumpy's name was Lawrence, but he preferred Larry. Stretch was Joey Rowe. And Twig's name was Thomas, not Tom. The two guys who knew each other were Sid and Adrian — they both wore braces and spoke without moving their lips . . . preppies from the word go. They were probably there for punishment. Probably went joy riding in one of their parents' mercedes, so to keep them out of trouble their parents signed them up for tennis lessons.

Probably bought them their own cars so they could get to class, too.

"Well, since this is a beginner's class, we'll start from the beginning," she said. A couple of us chuckled politely, just to make her feel good, but Sid and Adrian dropped their heads and groaned. They thought they were really special.

"You hold your racket as if you were shaking hands with it," she instructed, extending her racket and slowly gripping the handle finger by finger. We all mimicked her. Twig dropped his racket and almost fell over trying to retrieve it.

After a few pointers on swinging, we paired up. Sid and Adrian clung to each other and ran off to Court Four, the farthest from Ms. Allen. Dumpy, the short fat kid, and Twig, Mister Skin and Bones, partnered – *opposites attract.* And I had Stretch, the tall gooky kid who looked about as coordinated as a newborn colt.

"Just volley the ball back and forth," she directed. "Nothing fancy. See how many times you can put the ball across the net without stopping."

We stayed on Court One with Ms. Allen. Stretch had the tennis balls, and he took a couple of practice swings before striking the first one.

"That looks like good technique, Joey," said Ms. Allen.

"Thanks," said Stretch.

I could just picture him lofting the sucker into the cheap seats. He took a couple of more practice swings, more for Ms. Allen's benefit than his, I figured. And then he waved a ball into the air as if to say, "Here it comes."

Right, I thought, smirking to myself. You mean, There it goes.

Stretch, or Joey, struck the ball perfectly. It whipped just inches over the top of the net and landed dead center on my side. I was so shocked that I swatted at it and drilled the thing right into the entrance of the men's locker room.

Holy. What an idiot.

"Keep your eye on the ball," called Ms. Allen. "Watch it come into your racket head. And Scott, don't try to kill it."

I was ripping mad. Stretch didn't say a word. I would have jumped the net and strangled him if he had.

He practiced his swing again — which irritated the hell out of me — and then waved the stupid ball into the air. This time I kept my eyes focused and watched it come into my racket. Still, I couldn't get the feel of the swing. The ball struck the metal frame with a flat, dead sound. It wobbled pitifully over to Stretch's side just out of his reach. "Bet-ter," called Ms. Allen in a sing-song.

Right.

"Level off your swing," she said, demonstrating with a smooth stroke. "Watch it into your racket."

The ball flew. Again, a perfect hit by Stretch. I watched it float across the net. I controlled my swing — level and firm. Concentrated. *Pop.*

Perfect. The ball landed right in front of Stretch, but this time he launched it over Court Two, nearly decapitating a couple of women who were walking into the lounge.

"Sorry," he said, waving.

"Keep working at it." Ms. Allen turned to watch some of the other boys.

While Stretch ran off to retrieve balls, I watched an advanced class playing on the far courts. The kids there volleyed skillfully; the balls floated from one side of the court to the other. Their swings were powerful but controlled, and the sound of the racket hitting the ball was incredible — a beautiful solid *pop*, like the awesome *swish* of hitting all net on a twenty-footer or the perfect *thwack* of a lined soccer ball rippling the back of the net.

I couldn't keep my eyes off the advanced players. I studied their swings, the placement of their feet, the position of their free arms. As in every other sport, balance and speed made the difference. I leveled off my racket and took slow, precise swings.

I thought about Coach Hill's words from lacrosse, "Make your stick a part of you, like another arm." And then that feeling started to swell inside me, and the adrenaline began to pump. I felt as if I were in pre-game warm-ups — powerful, unstoppable, couldn't do anything wrong.

"Ready?" Stretch waved his stupid hand once again.

I nodded. Set myself. The ball floated across the net as I cross-stepped into position. I drew back my racket and swung through the ball – it lined back snapping the white top of the net and flipping into his court. Stretch couldn't return it. But I didn't care; I had the feel.

The better I got, the more Stretch fell apart. After a while he couldn't even serve the ball over the net. And he began to swear. Well, I suppose to him it was swearing. "This bleeping game." His face grew darker shades of red as he huffed about on his side of the court.

Finally, Ms. Allen stepped next to him and tried guiding his racket – it didn't work. Matter of fact, old Stretch stiffened up like the Tin Man on the *Wizard of Oz* when she reached around his waist.

"Relax," she said. "Come with me." Ms. Allen took Stretch to a practice wall with a white line painted on it net high. She gave the kid a basket of balls and guided him through the swing once again. Once he'd hit a few good ones, she came back to me.

"Okay, Scott. Let's volley."

She struck the first one firmly and right at me. I met it, but I hit the thing low and it slapped into the net. But the next one I returned.

"Good," she said. "Nice swing."

And then it began. Back and forth. Side to side. A rhythm, like a dance almost. Or when a soccer team begins to flow. No one thinks, really. It's like instinct. Passes come out of nowhere, and as my coach always said, "When it begins to click, it's as if the players are of one mind." The feeling grew inside me. After just two minutes or so of play, the sweat oozed out of my pores. I struggled to take a deep breath, and for the first time in weeks I felt like an athlete again.

"You're wonderful," she said after three long volleys. "You've played before."

"No. Never."

"Unbelievable," she said. "You're a natural." In the same breath Ms. Allen called Stretch back to the Court One.

Playing with Stretch was horrible. He got the ball across the net now, but there wasn't any rhythm to our game. We never volleyed over four or five times in a row, and every time he missed it, he'd whine a little or "swear." Then he'd apologize with his weasel voice.

The practice ended. Ms. Allen called all of us together on Court

One. "What a wonderful beginning. You must all feel very good. Watch some tennis on television – there's a good match on the sports channel on Wednesday evening at eight o'clock. If you can visualize yourself playing well, that's half the battle. I'll see you on Thursday."

As we headed to the locker room, Ms. Allen called my name. "You really have a great touch," she said stepping to my side. "You ought to challenge your mom. You'd give her a good match!"

I smiled. She had me hooked.

"See you Thursday."

I twirled my racket like a gunslinger as I walked into the shower room. The other guys were already soaping up as I peeled off my sweaty shirt and dragged down my shorts. I sat on the wooden bench to pull off my sneakers. I was totally wasted but psyched.

It felt good to be a jock again – to step into a locker room. I grabbed my towel and tip-toed over the cold tile into the gang shower and glanced at the other kids. Dumpy had rolls of fat and a tiny, wrinkled, miserable-looking penis with what looked to be three or four strands of pubic hair framing the thing. Twig, of course, was nothing but bone – scary to look at. Stretch kind of looked like a Christmas tree – a scrawny chest and wide, bony hips. Sid and Adrian had pretty athletic-looking bodies, but not toned. Too much partying, I figured.

The chemo hadn't gotten my muscles yet, so I kind of liked parading by all of these other guys.

"My feet are killing me," groaned Dumpy.

I looked at his rolls of fat and made a few silent suggestions.

"Man, she's incredible," said Sid.

"I know," returned Adrian confidently.

"Sure you do."

The two kids laughed. I slapped the silver button to the shower, tested the stream of water with my hand, and stepped forward when it turned warm. Incredible. I'd forgotten what it felt like to work out, and I'd forgotten how great a shower felt afterwards.

The other guys began leaving one by one. I closed my eyes, dropped my head, and breathed deeply. The water massaged the muscles of my neck and shoulders. It ran over my stomach, trickled down my legs. Leaning my hands against the white-tiled wall, I dropped my head further into the stream.

I felt strong and healthy – athletic. Something in my chest swelled with power, and I tingled all over. I hadn't felt like this in such a long time that I didn't want it to stop.

Tennis. I smiled and said the word out loud. I chuckled to myself. Then, I took a double take to make sure everyone had left. Last thing I needed was some guy telling the others that I was talking to myself in the shower. Never know where that would lead.

I couldn't wait for the next lesson and a chance to volley with Ms. Allen. And yes, I would challenge my mother to a match.

"Bring it on, Ma." I glanced back down toward the entrance with a big grin on my face – no one. I doused my head again. Lathered my hair with shampoo. "Tennis. No problem. Got it covered."

At first I thought it was some kind of bug on my arm, and I swiped at it. But as the water and soap ran out of my hair, I saw more and more. I felt it slithering over my shoulders.

I reached up, ran my fingers through my hair, and stepped back against the opposite wall. I stared at my hands and the strands of hair wedged neatly between each finger.

The chemo juice had struck.

My knees went cold. I stood absolutely still and wouldn't breathe.

My body felt as if it had let go of life.

I was sick again.

— 4 —

When I woke up the next morning, clumps of hair lay on my pillow. I patted my scalp and searched for bald spots. My fingers touched cold and a shiver ran down through my shoulders to the base of my spine. I hesitated and then slowly brushed at my hair. More let loose and fell onto my shoulders and onto the white sheets of my bed and my pillowcase.

I dropped my head into my hands and cried. My body shook all over. I wanted to scream, but was afraid of the noise.

Now it was real. Before, my cancer hadn't been one hundred percent there. I could fake it. I could be healthy if I wanted. I could ignore the way I felt and concentrate on anything else. The only time I really knew for sure that I was sick was when I went into outpatient for treatments.

There, it was real. There, I felt out of control. In the hospital, people were always touching me. They were always putting stuff inside me and jabbing me with needles. I felt naked even when I had all my clothes on.

The hospital was a strange place. A lot of people had a distant look about them. I hated that look. It scared me.

Everyone joked a lot in the hospital, too. The nurses flirted with me, pinched my cheeks, ran their hands across my thigh, asked me what I was doing on Saturday night. They made me blush, got me laughing, took my mind off the needles and the smells and the thirty percent who died.

But still, between the laughter and the smiles, between the jokes and the flirting invitations, that look was always there. It was something in their eyes — not exactly like the "kid-with-cancer" stare that I faced at school — this was a distant look, something that went on forever. It made me feel far away. People in the healthy world didn't seem to have that look.

The older nurses and doctors didn't have it either; I figured they had learned how to hide it. When I stared into their eyes, I knew they liked me and I knew they cared, but they never got too close.

The young ones, the nurses fresh out of school or the energetic interns, people not a whole lot older than me, their eyes screamed *the look*. They tried to hide it with jokes and stuff, but their eyes always told the truth.

As I sat in bed, I pulled my legs into my chest and wrapped my arms around them. I didn't move. I closed my eyes and drew my thoughts inward, dropping my head to my knees. I always did this when I was scared and feeling alone. Used to be I would wake up in the middle of the night when I was ten or eleven years old and think about my parents and the day they would die. Back when I was five or six, I'd go right into their room and crawl into their bed and snuggle, but boys of ten or eleven didn't go whimpering into their parents' bedroom in the middle of the night because they'd had a dream. That's when I discovered that curling up into a ball made me feel better, as if someone were with me, as if someone were holding me tight.

I could hear my mother and my father talking in the hallway; they were whispering, so I figured they were discussing me. I brushed the hair on my pillow into a pile and scooped it into the waste basket next to my bed. Then I dropped a couple of tissues on top to cover the evidence.

I hadn't told them about my hair the night before, and I figured they hadn't noticed. But now they were sure to see.

There was a knock at my door and my mother's soft voice. "Scott, it's time to get up. It's six thirty. Rise and shine." The door creaked open and she poked her head in. "Good morning."

I was still sitting up in bed, cradling my head, and trying to cover my hair. It didn't work.

"Your hair?" She stepped inside my room.

I nodded, closed my eyes and tightened my lips. I didn't want her to see me. I didn't want anyone to see.

For a moment she stood silent and still. I figured it wouldn't take long for her to come over and sit on the edge of my bed and say all the things I didn't want to hear. I couldn't have been more wrong.

"I thought you were going to get away with it. I thought that if anyone were going to keep his hair it would be you," she said. "Well, how do you want to handle it? You could wear a cap to school today, or you could go for broke and I could cut it all off."

Her words stung. Hit home. I couldn't believe what she had said or how she had said it. So matter of factly, so coldly, as if asking what I wanted for breakfast. I closed my eyes tighter.

"Let's have a look."

"Ma," I groaned, raising my head slowly but not looking at her. Finally, I took away my hands. I wanted to look at her. Part of me wanted to get up and run to her and have her hold me. But I sat there, alone.

"That doesn't look so bad," she said, moving to my side.

I knew she was supposed to say that. Even so, it made me feel a bit better, but then she reached out and ran her fingers through my hair, gently pulling at it. I could feel the strands coming out, and I pushed her hand away. I didn't want to be touched.

"So, what do you think? A cap? Do I take out the clippers?"

This didn't sound like my mother. Her words wiped me out and drilled at my stomach until it felt hollow. I could barely find the strength to whisper, "I'm staying at home today. My stomach's upset."

She stared at me for a moment searching for the right words. "I'm sorry," she whispered, sounding more like my mother, her voice soft and caring.

Of course she knew quite well that I could have gone to school. But she understood. "I'll get you something," she said. "And why don't you think about what you want to do with your hair."

I dropped my head again and wrapped my arms around my legs as she left the room.

When my mother came back with the stomach medicine, her face was stern, her lips tight. But what I noticed most were her eyes. She did all she could to keep them turned away from me. But no use. She'd been crying. And for all her tough talk, I knew she couldn't stand this anymore than I.

For most of that day I stayed home in my bedroom. I said little. I stared at myself in the mirror a lot, and every few minutes I pulled at my hair, testing, to see if maybe, just maybe, some of it would stay. But each time I yanked, another clump fell free. When I looked in the mirror, it was weird. I didn't look like me. It was as if I had on a Halloween wig.

My mother never mentioned the cap or the clippers again that day, and she actually left for a few hours to go and play tennis. As I look back now, I'm sure she didn't want to go, but she knew the fight was mine and mine alone.

That evening I got my act together and put on my Red Sox hat. That hat was my pride and joy. I'd won it from my father a few years back during a three-day Red Sox/Yankees series.

"Nice hat," said my father as I strode into the kitchen. As a part of the bet, my father wasn't allowed to dump on the Red Sox anymore. That killed him. He hated them . . . "Stick a fork in the good old Sox, I think they're done!"

The bet was all my mother's idea. She couldn't stand our constant bickering – he for the Pinstripes and me for the Sox. So she came up with this idea. Once and for all, whichever team won this three-game series, the loser would have to buy the winner a hat and both would promise never to ridicule the other's team again. It came down to the last game and the ninth inning – one swing later my father never said another crummy word about "The Boston Chokers" and I had a new hat.

"How are you?" asked my father, touching his own hair.

"I'm getting used to it."

"Today at work I couldn't stop thinking about you and how brave you are. I thought about how I would have handled this at your age – I wasn't sure," he said softly. "But I am sure about one thing: you really are something, Scott."

My father's words embarrassed me. I waited expecting him to take it back, to temper his words somehow or to joke. But he didn't, and my mother put her hand on his arm.

My father had been a great athlete in high school and college. I'd never seen him afraid of anything ever. He still played in a basketball league with guys fifteen years younger than he was. And although he wasn't quite as quick as they were, he never let up. My dad was tough.

My mother slid her arm around his shoulders. "Like father, like son."

"And like mother," whispered my dad.

None of us said anything for the longest time. Even so, I felt good. Finally, as if the answer had been there all along, I said, "I guess I'd like you to cut my hair. I'll wear my hat tomorrow to school."

"Okay." My mother's cheery voice lifted my spirits. "But why don't we run out tonight and get you a new hat?"

"No way!" I laughed putting my hand to the brim. "This is my good luck hat – I'm going to have this puppy forever."

I looked over at my dad as he backed out of the kitchen. I knew that he was about to cry.

— 5 —

No one at school except Kevin said a word about my hair. They sneaked little glances at me when I wasn't looking, but I knew. I didn't have to see. I could feel their eyes, and even though I couldn't make out their words, I knew what they were saying. And I knew they felt awkward and uncomfortable around me.

I had wished everyone could be like Kevin. Sometimes he went overboard though, like at the end of the day when he called me "Cue ball." But most of the time it was good to have someone being up front and unafraid.

I hated the silence and the frightened stares of my classmates. At home I'd turn on the television, the stereo, anything that made noise . . . I just didn't want to be left alone in the silence. I wished I could do the same in school.

That first hairless day back at school I ended up behind Lori James in the lunch line. She was yapping away with a friend of hers as they moved past the milk cooler. Finally, she turned around and caught a glimpse of me. Her smile vanished, and I thought I could sense her fear like that day in the library.

I wanted to say something to her, but she never looked back again. And I could see her shoulders getting smaller, caving in, as she moved quickly through the line, escaping.

At tennis that afternoon, Ms. Allen partnered with me. Joey Rowe – good old Stretch – had decided that tennis just wasn't his game. Fair enough, I thought.

"Are you losing your hair?" she asked, standing on the other side of the net pointing at my Red Sox hat.

"Yup."

"Well, at least you have your good looks!"

"Right," I scoffed.

And that was it: Time to play. She held up a ball and backed away. In some ways Barbara Allen was a lot like Kevin. She wasn't afraid to hit stuff head on. She didn't have that look, either. And it wasn't because she didn't care, I knew that. Like Kevin, Ms. Allen knew that I didn't need to dwell on being sick. She made me feel normal and healthy.

We volleyed for a few minutes. I was confident and composed; I could have played forever. My legs felt strong, my eyes focused. It was as if I'd played this game my whole life. But then, who was I kidding? She was serving up the ball like a watermelon so anyone could have returned it. But I didn't care — I just wanted to play.

At first, I wasn't sure if I'd heard the words correctly. I couldn't imagine anyone using *those* words out loud. But then, amid the echoes and the bouncing balls, the grunts and groans, I was sure.

"Excuse me," said Ms. Allen striding off toward Sid and Adrian. "Seems like they're having some problems."

Problems. Right. They were whipping the ball at one another, swearing up a storm as they ducked the other's attack. Some of the balls flew into adjacent courts and one of them nailed Twig. I thought it was going to bowl him over as he staggered around rubbing his arm as if he'd just been shot.

"Okay, Guys!"

Sid looked at Ms. Allen with an expression that screamed *What's the big deal?* Adrian was a bit more subdued, and he stood politely as the two of them got reamed out. I couldn't hear a word Ms. Allen said, but she had obviously done a good job because the two boys lowered their heads by degrees like scolded dogs.

When she came back, her face was flushed, but her voice was calm. "Sometimes," she moaned, shaking her head then looking up at me. "I want you to play with one of the boys from the advanced class. It will be good for you." And before I could muster a protest, she was walking across the complex and waving at a boy in the far court.

Eric was a tall, slender blonde-headed kid whose gray-blue eyes were serious and made him seem older than he was. He had a pug nose and a sprinkling of freckles on his cheeks. His easy smile and cock of the head made me like him immediately.

"Eric Burke. Scott Cinader," introduced Ms. Allen.

I was horrible at introductions and stared at my sneakers as I shook his hand. My father had always said, "Look'em right square in the eye and shake so they'll know you're there."

Well, I slid my hand into his as if the life had left my arm, and he grabbed me as if he was going to drag me away. I'll never forget that handshake. Never. It was over in an instant, as if Eric knew I was uncomfortable.

"Good to meet you, Scott," he said in a nasally voice.

Ms. Allen stepped between us. "Now listen, Eric. It's Scott's second day, but he's a natural. Keep an eye on his feet and his racket positioning."

"Sure, Barbara. I'll do my best."

I couldn't believe that he had called her *Barbara*, as if they were the same age. I couldn't believe how comfortable he was with her. At first I thought that maybe I'd misread him – that maybe he was cocky and thought he was special. The whiz kid brought down to the "lower courts" to babysit some loser.

But I discovered quickly that Eric wasn't anything like that. Not at all.

"You're kidding, right?" he shouted as he returned one of my crossing shots. "How long you been playing?"

"A couple of days."

"Sure."

"Seriously, I usually play basketball in the winter. I just started playing this on Tuesday."

"Okay. Whatever."

I knew that he believed me and was just playing it through. I liked the attention, and I liked that he thought I was good, too.

"All set?" he asked, holding a ball in the air.

I nodded.

One thing was for sure – Eric could play. He was an athlete, though thinly built. He moved about the court a lot like Danny Rouleau did playing basketball. His swing was pure and quick and natural. The sound the ball made off of his racket – that solid *pop* – was a special sound, rich and deep as it echoed off the wall behind me and the ceiling above.

I envied Eric and that sound. Tried to move as he moved. Watched his racket. His eyes. The way he stood just before he served up the ball. The way he held the racket as he waited for me to deliver. I knew then that I wanted to master this game. That I wanted to know what it felt like to be in command.

At break, we sat against the wall and shot cups of water. I was dripping with sweat, but Eric showed no sign of work. Was he bored? And then out of nowhere . . .

"Chemotherapy?" He touched his own hair as he looked at my baseball cap and the bald spots showing beneath.

I'm sure my eyes betrayed me. I couldn't believe how he just said it. I nodded.

"What kind of cancer is it?"

Holy. There was a casualness in his voice, but it was not careless. I could tell that he was concerned. "I have this thing growing in my chest."

"How are the treatments going?"

"Good, so far. It's getting smaller."

"Great. I'm really happy for you."

He looked into my eyes so intently that I felt stronger. His voice lifted me up, took hold of me as if somehow I was being healed at that very moment.

* * *

That night, after homework, I watched my mother's tennis video for nearly two hours. Winding, rewinding. Watching serves, checking out backhands, swinging my own racket with all the precision I could muster.

Then, in front of the mirror, I practiced shaking hands.

– 6 –

Of all the crazy things that Kevin had ever done, this was certainly the craziest. Even his Challenge couldn't top this, and that was a legend at St. John's.

The Challenge was pretty simple. Kevin announced in the cafeteria at our table that for a buck apiece we could put anything edible into his half glass of chocolate milk. Then, he would drink it. There were seven of us sitting together, and before you could draw a second breath, the dollar bills were flying.

I dropped in a dark red slice of slimy tomato. K.J. poured in some cold turkey soup – he scraped the white ring of fat off the edge of the bowl and put that in just for good measure. Derek added orange juice which curdled the milk. Scot shook in some salt – Matt some pepper. But when Jon chewed up a mouthful of green peas and spit them in, drool and all, we figured all bets were off.

Wrong.

Kevin lifted the glass above eye level and gently swirled it a couple of times. Then, balancing the glass between his thumb and forefinger, as if he were about to sip a fine wine, he lowered the concoction to his lips and slowly drank every – single – drop.

"Delicious."

He wiped his lips and grabbed the money from the middle of the table as Jon lurched into a sprint and hit the boys room just in time to power barf in and around the first urinal. As for me, I felt the juices of my stomach creeping into the back of my throat. I sat very still, closed my eyes, and swallowed cautiously several times.

That was Kevin's Challenge, but this was even better, at least for me. On my second hairless day in school, a small crowd in homeroom was gathered in the back near Kevin's desk. At first, I couldn't see anything except arms and shoulders, but then people started to move, and there he was, large as life. Boston Red Sox cap. Bald as a cue ball. My best friend, Kevin.

"Pretty cool, huh?" he asked, flipping off his hat and rubbing his shaved scalp.

"You're nuts."

"Hey, you kidding? No more shampoo. No more blow dryers. Hell, I should have thought of this years ago.

I stared at him and shook my head, eyes closed, disbelieving.

"Hey, Cinader, relax. And remember: there ain't no rule that says you ain't cool without hair."

There ain't no rule that says you ain't cool without hair.

That day, my clone Kevin and I sneaked out of the library into the auditorium as we had many times before. Kevin had "acquired" a key to the place (I never asked) so we could escape whenever the school walls began to close in or when we just felt like doing something against the rules. Sometimes we'd take a nap; other times we'd just sit and talk. Whatever, it was our place.

He rolled onto the carpeted floor while I threw my legs over the seat in front of me. We sat quietly in the shadows cast by the stage-door light. Kevin shifted and stretched a couple of times while I slumped deeper into my seat, finding just the right position for my legs as they dangled over the chair in front of me.

Without warning, Kevin grunted – half giggle, half serious. It was as if he had just remembered something not quite important enough to get upset about.

"What's up?"

"Oh, I was just thinking about The Tribe." His voice sounded flat and removed, no sign of laughter, nothing to remind me of Kevin. The wistful, absent sound of his voice made me nervous, and for a brief moment the thought came to me that perhaps he regretted having shaved his head. That I wasn't worth it. That –

"Boy, those were the days." His voice grew stronger now and his face lightened. "Spying on Michael and Peggy."

Relieved, I joined in. "The hide-out."

"K.J.'s *Playboys*."

"Incredible."

And then together we both laughed, "The Mosquito Test."

"Ha! Bugs-R-Us!" Kevin tossed back his head in delight and I remembered those days when nothing was more important than The Tribe.

To become a member of The Brotherhood of the Tribe, a kid had to pass The Mosquito Test. Like The Challenge, The Test was Kevin's idea all the way. And like The Challenge, The Mosquito Test was painfully simple. Painfully.

Prospective members were led into the deepest woods outside of town next to a swampy bog. There, the boy – no girls were ever let into The Brotherhood – was told to strip down to his underwear and sit on a log for ten minutes. There was only one rule: you could not move. Not a finger. (In Maine, May and June are the height of black fly and mosquito season – we always held the test some time during those 60 days.)

For the first few moments – before the tiny bugs had sensed their naked prey – some initiates would sit and smile nervously, wondering, hoping that all they had heard about The Test was just pumped-up talk. Others, the bolder ones, would mouth off a bit. "This is nothing." "Big test." But within a couple of minutes, their talk stopped dead as what seemed to be thousands of prickly, blood-sucking bugs began to settle in. It was then that every kid knew the true meaning of torture.

Most couldn't handle it. They'd fight off the tiny stings and bites for three minutes – perhaps four. Then they'd stumble off the log screaming and slapping and swearing. They'd grab their clothes and run toward town. They never looked back. Most of those kids – their egos as welted as their skin – wouldn't be heard from for days.

As for those few who withstood the trial, they were welcomed into a select group and were given all the rights and privileges of The Brotherhood of the Tribe: use of the secret cabin near the bog, unlimited pawing of K.J.'s magazines, and nightly jaunts of intrigue, adventure, or sex (watching K.J.'s brother Michael and his girlfriend, Peggy, *doing it* in the back seat of his car).

That day in school I began to feel normal again. I never once felt that horrible look of fright or pity from any of the kids at St. John's. I'm sure they were there, but I just didn't notice. I got bawled out in history by Mr. Wood for talking. "Mr. Cinader, do you think you could tend to business?" And K.J. laced me in the arm as I strode down the hallway between classes. It wasn't a friendly, how-ya-doing tap, but a full blown slug that rocked me into the lockers. I felt it for days, and I loved that pain as much as anything.

That afternoon at two o'clock, my mother and I went to The Racket. I couldn't believe how excited I was about the prospect of playing her. Usually, whenever I did something "athletic" with my mother – horseshoes, badminton, whiffle ball – it was more out of obligation than anything else. But not that day; I was psyched, as if it were a night match in soccer against our arch rivals, The Cougars of Dixmont.

When we arrived, Barbara Allen and another woman were battling on Court One. And I mean battling. It was incredible. I'd never seen two women go at it like this – sweating, groaning, and their faces as fierce and ferocious as any guy's. Only a few of the girls at school that I knew competed anything like this. Most of them squealed and squeaked and shied away from a good fight. A few of the girls on the basketball team were game tough, but because their teammates weren't, it kind of ruined it for the rest. But even so, none of them could compare to Ms. Allen and this other woman. This was a war.

My mother and I were assigned Court Seven. We stretched a bit and then began to volley. Watching my mother's video tape and practicing my stroke in the living room had paid off some. I felt smooth and more balanced – my racket moved through the ball crisply, and that solid, telling *pop* echoed in the air on almost every strike. Most of all, I felt at home on the court.

"Oh my, Scott. I wish I had started you when you were a little boy," she said. "You'd probably be a professional player. This is amazing."

"Do you think it's too late for me to get good?" I asked, my voice weak and cracking, not sure if I really wanted to hear her response.

My mother stepped up to the net and looked right into my eyes. "You already are good."

"No, you know what I mean."

"Listen, at the rate you're improving . . ."

"Didn't I tell you he was something?" Barbara Allen walked up to the net with a towel draped over her shoulders and a water bottle cradled in her hands.

"I just don't believe it." My mother moved toward the net. "I feel so guilty. I should have started him years ago."

I looked quickly toward Ms. Allen hoping to hear it wasn't too late. Praying that I hadn't missed my chance.

"Well, no sense worrying about that. Who knows, he might have gotten bored with it and quit by now."

"I suppose you're right."

"And you, Mister. You're going to have to move up to an advanced class. You're just too good. Time to jump in with the big boys."

"Fine by me."

"I hope so, because it's not going to be a picnic. You're going to get kicked around a lot. Some of these kids like Eric can play some real hot tennis."

"He's in the class?"

"Yes."

"Good."

"I hope you say that after you play him. He's a nice kid, but he's an animal in a match."

"No problem."

A smile came to my mother's face as I spoke. She used to get after me for being too confident. "Pride goeth before a fall," she'd preach. A lot of times I'd screw up somehow just after she'd warned me about my cockiness. But this day I could tell she loved seeing the old fire resurface.

By the time we had left The Racket at four o'clock, I was exhausted. Ms. Allen had joined in and we played Canadian Doubles, two against one, so I could work on my serve and backhand. Going against my mother and her was hard work, but I would have played until I dropped. I listened carefully to their suggestions and made adjustments to my game. I could feel myself getting better — I could sense I was growing stronger. On the drive home my body felt like one gigantic throb. I loved the feeling. My mother's talk was quick and animated; I could tell that she was enjoying the fact that I had taken to her game. And I knew she savored what Ms. Allen had said at the end of our match: "Watch out. This young man is dangerous."

We stopped at the intersection of Grand and Penobscot. Suddenly, all the cars from every direction except one came to a stop. A long, black wagon with flags on either side of its hood and its high beams on drove slowly through the intersection. The car was filled with flowers. Behind it, a shiny black hearse.

I stared at the rich brown of the coffin in the back and felt my breath being taken away, as if someone had punched me in the solar plexus. A line of cars filed through the intersection, each with a black and white flag – Funeral – attached to its aerial. Their high beams sliced the twilight of this dismal winter's day.

I stared at the mourners. Some were stone-faced and pale, frightening to look at, death-like themselves. But those in the cars farther back wore smiles as if they were going to a wedding reception or some sort of dance. I could not believe it.

With each passing car, my pain grew. Wild thoughts dashed through my mind. Would my friends laugh in my funeral procession? Would anyone really care if I died? Who'd remember me?

And like The Mosquito Test, the last few cars to pass like the last few seconds of stinging agony seemed to take a lifetime.

— 7 —

I stood near Court One and could see Eric stretching on the other side of the complex. He was deliberate. Methodical. Serious. A couple of the kids in the advanced class messed around. They drove tennis balls at one another while they waited for Jack Fredericks, the other pro at The Racket.

It took me a couple of moments to get up enough guts to join Eric. As I walked across the courts, a ball whipped my head around. A bleached-blonde kid waved timidly. I waved back and held up my thumb and forefinger to show him just how close it had been.

"Sorry about that!" shouted the boy.

"It's okay."

Eric listened to a Walkman. His eyes were closed as he lay back with his lower legs tucked beneath him in a painful looking stretch. I sat down nearby, flipped one leg up under my butt and leaned back looking at the ceiling. My quad burned a little and I could feel a gentle, warm sensation.

"Feels great, doesn't it?" Eric slid the earphones down to his shoulders.

"I love it."

"You ever try stretching to music?"

"Unh-unh."

"It's awesome. You've got to try it."

"What are you listening to?"

"A prelude by Chopin."

I'd heard of Chopin. Knew it was some kind of classical stuff. Music that my mother listened to on Sunday mornings while she read the newspaper. The kind of music that drove my father and me out onto our driveway basketball court every Sunday without fail.

"Ever listen to Chopin?"

"I don't think so."

"Do you like classical music?"

"Well, a little." *Very little.*

"I never did until my friend Brian turned me on to it a while back. I still like rock, but sometimes classical works better for what I'm doing."

I switched legs. Eric changed positions.

"Want to listen? I've got an extra set of earphones."

"Sure."

He rummaged through his gym bag and found the other set. "Just lie back and go with it," he said, handing them over. "I think about a pond in the middle of the forest – crystal clear water, no waves at all, just glass."

"Okay." *A pond in the middle of a forest?* When the music began, I felt self-conscious, as if everyone in the place was staring at me. I tried to look "into" it. I closed my eyes – didn't want to hurt Eric's feelings. But all I could hear was the noise from the courts – kids screaming, balls rebounding off walls, and the low steady hum of forced heat from the duct works overhead.

I peeked over toward Eric and saw him take hold of the cassette player and turn up the volume. Most of the outside noise disappeared then. My head filled with the soft, airy piano music that whispered in my ear.

I'm not sure what it was exactly, but in a couple of moments I felt as if I was being taken away. I felt as if I was riding on the notes. Drifting out of the courts. It was the weirdest sensation, because every once in a while I could hear the noise from the tennis courts. It was as if I were slingshotting back and forth from some place out in space and then back to the courts again. The longer I listened, the more the music took hold.

At one point I stood on top of Tumbledown Mountain near the village of Weld, looking out over the lake and across miles of hilly woods to the White Mountains in New Hampshire. I could actually feel the wind in my face and smell the clean air of the mountain top. Suddenly, it was like those wonderful flying dreams I'd had when I was young – soaring out over the mountains, diving into the valleys and skimming inches above the lake.

Flying.

Soaring.

Like looking through gauze.

A touch.

No music. Another touch. My insides jumped – roller coaster stuff – I looked around.

"You were *gone*." Eric smiled, his face beaming.

It was like those times when you fall asleep in the late afternoon and wake up not knowing whether it's the next morning or the next year.

"I can't believe it. One minute I was lying there thinking 'This is really stupid,' and then I'm buzzing around the mountains."

"Great stuff, huh?"

"Incredible."

"Better than a cheap movie and an ugly date!"

It took me a moment, then . . . "Yeah. Really. It's like getting hypnotized, you know?"

"Yeah."

"No one will believe it."

"You're right. No one."

Eric's words sounded strangely sad. I wanted to say something to him, but I didn't know what. Anyway, he was the tennis star, what could I say to him? He certainly didn't need me. Just then, Jack Fredericks arrived.

Mr. Fredericks was a big man with brown hair and a ruddy complexion. I could tell from the way he stood that he was a no-nonsense kind of guy. He looked strict like Mr. Greenleaf, my soccer coach. Both had a hardness in their eyes, a hint of distaste, as if they had better things to do with their time than bother with teenagers. Mr. Fredericks, like Coach Greenleaf, made me nervous.

"Has everyone stretched?"

All the guys nodded. Lying certainly looked easier than facing this guy's wrath.

"Good. Let's volley for a few minutes."

We began pairing up.

"Hold it!" His voice froze us. "Pay attention to your technique. Forget the power behind your stroke. Concentrate on the perfect swing."

Eric moved next to the blonde-headed kid who had almost taken my head off, and the rest of the guys were doubled, too. So there I stood. Some of the kids looked at me – stared, really. Of course everyone knew I had cancer; I'm sure the word had spread instantly through the locker room. And if they hadn't heard officially, it didn't take a brain surgeon to see that I didn't have any hair beneath my Red Sox cap.

The next thing I knew . . .

"With me," said Fredericks, pointing his finger.

Holy. A tryout?

We walked to Court Three. On the way he snapped at a couple of guys reminding them of the assignment. "Forget the power – think technique." The next thing I knew we were facing each other on opposite sides of the court, and he was waving a ball into the air . . . that was it.

The ball he served up was perfect: not too hard, not too soft. I didn't have time to think. I just swung. My return was solid. Pretty close to the net and right down the center. All right, I thought. I can handle this.

But he caught the ball. He reached out with his freehand and caught the ball.

As Fredericks walked toward the net, I felt myself inching backwards.

"Listen. You've got to move your feet to get into position. Your swing has to be level." He demonstrated in slow motion. "Play the ball to the back of the court – play it deep."

"Okay."

He turned and walked away. Then, almost as if he could hear my heart pounding and my stomach doing loop the loops, Fredericks turned around, his head tilted and a sparkle in his eye. "And for pete's sake, relax."

And I did. After awhile. Playing with Fredericks was kind of like playing with Ms. Allen. There was a rhythm. The ball floated and it always seemed perfectly placed for me to hit. When I played with them,

I didn't have to think about my arms or my legs – things just fell into place, and all I had to do was concentrate on the ball and my racket.

Eric was to play off against the bleached-blonde kid who almost nailed me. The winner would represent The Racket in the fifteen and sixteen-year-old division of a city-wide singles tournament. I stayed after class with a few of the guys to watch the three-set match. They kept joking about "the execution," "the massacre."

"I'll give Vladie two points a game," said one.

"Too generous. Straight sets – fifteen points max for Vladie."

"Whatever. It won't be a pretty sight."

Vladimir Brandeis won the toss and chose to serve. I was surprised that the guys didn't give him more of a chance because his two practice serves scorched into Eric's court.

"Nice serves, Vladie," called Eric, not making any attempt to return them.

The boy raised his racket and smiled.

I thought it was pretty neat how friendly the two guys were. It couldn't be that way in some sports. Hate, or something close to it, had a lot to do with how hard you played – whether you gave the extra – whether you won or loss. And these two guys didn't hate each other. It would have been like Kevin and me going one-on-one. We would have knocked each other around a little but that would be about it.

They played hard from the very start. Their faces were as intense as Ms. Allen's in her match the night before. But the most amazing thing was how fast the ball flew. I couldn't believe it. I'd seen tennis on television, but you couldn't tell how fast the ball was going. Sitting courtside you got a whole different perspective.

Vladie held serve and won the first game. The guys couldn't believe it.

"This is a first," said one.

"And a last . . ."

When they switched sides, I knew then that something was wrong. Vladie smiled and put his hand on Eric's shoulder as they passed at the net, but Eric looked straight ahead. Didn't say a word. He looked nothing like the kid that had listened to Chopin with me. Now he looked like a guy who was about to kill.

Each point was serious. Dead serious. Vladie tried a couple of times to laugh or to crack a joke, but Eric didn't budge. Then, it happened.

"You sure about that?" asked Eric pointedly, staring hard at the line after a close one.

"Positive, Eric," answered Vladie, his voice giving way.

"Looked to me as if it caught the line."

"Honest, Eric. It was out."

I couldn't believe it. Eric stood his ground at the net. He stared at the line, then glared at Vladie. It almost looked as if Eric was going to jump the net and tackle the kid.

"Ready?" Vladie's voice sounded weak and unsure.

Eric turned away and moved to the back of the court. His eyes were wild. Part of me wanted to get up and get out of there. Part of me wanted to stay and watch the tennis, half hoping that this was just a big act and they'd start laughing any minute.

Neither of them laughed.

Eric won the first set 6 - 4. It was a great battle, and the games were close. But the second set was a different story. Eric completely annihilated Vladie. He didn't give him a chance. He drove every ball hard and fast and deep, from one side of the court to the other, and then he finished off the blonde kid with brutal accuracy.

The thing that got me the most was Eric's face. His eyes. They looked vicious, savage, like someone starving to death.

And then the end of the match. Eric was up 5 - 1 in games and 30 - Love in this game. He had frozen Vladie dead center and had a high bouncing ball coming right down to his racket. He could have drilled the thing to either line, but instead, he aimed right for the kid. Vladie tried to skip back out of the way, but the ball thumped him in the chest. He ended up tripping and hitting the floor so hard that I turned away out of instinct.

"You okay?" asked Eric coming to the net.

But his words were hollow. I could tell he didn't care. He only cared about the win and making it to the tournament.

I turned and walked toward the locker room as Eric served.

Pop Pop Pop
Then, like a gunshot in the distance, a killer smash.
I never looked back.
I knew that Vladie was dead, and that Eric had made the kill.

— 8 —

"It's like The Tribe," said Kevin, poking his nose over the top of the book.

"Yeah. But The Mosquito Test was a lot worse than jumping off that stupid tree into the water," I said.

"Oh, no doubt."

We were sprawled out on the auditorium floor reading *A Separate Peace*. I knew that Kevin was thinking that Finny and Gene were kind of like us. That their Super Suicide Society of the Summer Session sounded like The Tribe and our summers of raids and wars and spying on anyone we could find. I knew because I was thinking the same thing.

"I love this book as much as *The Chocolate War*," I said.

"I know. I hate having it end. Chapter 11. Crap."

"Elmer was right. This book is the best."

"Abso-frigging-lutely." Kevin put his book down and looked dreamily toward the far wall. "Remember Elmer's test?"

"Of course," I chuckled. "Who could forget that? I remember how you stuck up for him at the bid meeting, too. What'd you say? 'I don't care if he is fat. I like him and I want him in.'"

Kevin laughed. "No one would say that to him now."

"No way."

Elmer was on the wrestling team with Kevin. Six-foot-six, 250-pound Elmer Mawhinny was also an all-state football player and a state champion shot putter. He didn't look anything like that when he took The Test. At eleven years old, he was a roly-poly kid no one paid much attention to. Even so, Elmer was always there. Quiet. Unassuming. Someone you could count on for right field in baseball or to carry the backpack for one of our adventures into the deep woods far beyond our cabin. In high school Elmer shot up, thinned out, and his round face matured. He was handsome, an honors student, and one of the nicest and most popular guys at St. John's.

"That was something else," said Kevin. "None of us took the test like Elmer."

"Mosquitoes!"

"Frigging thousands of them."

"Covered."

"And he didn't blink. Nothing. Frigging guy looked like a statue."

"I can still see him sitting there in that trance. And we kept spraying insect repellent all over us. A wicked year for bugs."

"Frigging incredible."

That said it all. We fell back into our books and began to read. We had to finish for English class that afternoon, but there was no way either one of us was going to rush. We loved this book for the memories it brought back.

I wrapped my eyes around each word, savored them. I hated the thought of it ending, of losing Finny and Gene forever. That was the worst part of reading a good book – it always ended. The friends I'd made out of the characters disappeared.

I even turned the pages slowly and took the time to press each one flat. A ritual of sorts. A sign of respect for a book that I loved. And back then, I didn't love many books. Suddenly, those words.

Your friend is dead.

I read the sentence again.

Finny had died.

And from a stupid broken leg!

I sat quietly, feeling the rage building inside me. How could a kid die from a broken leg? I looked over at Kevin. I knew he was on the same page because we had played a game of turning the pages at the same time.

His head bowed, and then, after a long moment, he glanced toward me with eyes that sliced the dim light of the auditorium.

There wouldn't be any jokes this time.

And neither of us read another word that day.

— 9 —

Eric didn't show up for tennis over the next couple of weeks. Vladie said that he was sick — I couldn't have been happier. There wasn't any doubt in my mind after watching him play against Vladie that Eric was a lying, two-faced prick, and I didn't want to have a thing to do with him.

I played as hard as I could over those next few weeks. Some days I felt tough and healthy. Some days I didn't. On chemo days, when the nausea medicine worked, I stayed at home and watched tennis videos and listened to psych-up music, never any of that classical crap. Piano music reminded me of Eric, and Eric made me sick.

At school I took naps in the nurse's office during fourth or fifth period so I could keep rested for tennis in the afternoon. I figured missing English or math was a good trade off, and I joked with Kevin that there were a few advantages to having cancer. Very few.

During those first couple of weeks at The Racket, I began to beat my mother consistently. The matches were grueling — nothing like any of our other mother and son contests. These were out and out battles that usually came down to the last couple of points.

Playing against my mother helped me see another side of her. Most of the time she wasn't my mother during a match — she played hard points against me and never let up, driving the ball deep into the court or deadening it to the base of the net so I'd have to sprint. My mother hated losing; after all, she had played for years and tennis was her game. But underneath her disappointment at losing I knew she was pleased to see the fight growing in me.

Vladie Brandeis became my new partner at lessons. Vladie was good. Better than I had first thought after seeing him get dismantled by Eric. When he hit the ball, it curved and spun, almost danced in the air.

I never knew what it was going to do. Sometimes the bounce didn't really bounce at all. Sometimes the ball actually went backwards, as if Vladie had an invisible string attached to it. When the moment was right, he'd yank it back and I'd stumble around like some kind of idiot. Other times, the thing would take off like one of those superballs and fly past me as if it had been fired from a howitzer.

Yes, Vladie Brandeis could play, and he was a good guy, too. He only used his tricks when I got cocky. And then it was just a gentle reminder; it didn't take much to show me who the boss was on the court, who the real player was.

I couldn't believe the reception Eric got the day that he returned to lessons. Even Vladie was all over him as if the kid had come back from the dead. But he hadn't. Pneumonia. Just a super cold. Big frigging deal.

He didn't look too good, though; in fact, he looked as if he'd been mainlining chemo juice: his face chalk white and his skin drawn tight. But even so, sick as he had been, I didn't think he deserved that much of a welcome.

"Okay, okay. Let's get to work," said Fredericks, breaking up the reunion. "Pair up and volley."

I wandered over next to Vladie. "Ready?"

"Sure. But let's triple up with Eric."

I didn't say a thing.

Vladie maneuvered through a couple of kids and grabbed Eric's shirt sleeve. "Come on, Sick Boy. Time to get your butt kicked."

Eric wrinkled his nose and broke into his sickening wide grin. "Canadian doubles?"

"Yup. With Scott."

"Terrific."

Terrific. I wanted to puke, and when Eric tapped me on the butt with his racket, I couldn't look his way. This guy could turn it on and off at will. A phony. I hated him. Two-faced all the way.

We moved to Court Eight at the far end of the complex. Vladie and Eric partnered, mainly because I jetted to the other side of the court and held up my hand like a traffic cop signaling them to stay put.

We volleyed. Within a few minutes my anger melted with the rhythm of play. Some days on the court I could tell if I was going to be on; something in the way I moved my feet. Some days the ball looked bigger as it crossed the net; those were the days that tennis gave me strength.

I played the best I had in days. My backhand snapped. The movement of the ball started to play tricks with Vladie and Eric, leaving them off-balanced and fooled. I was in control.

"Wow! You sure have come a long way." Eric stepped up to the net. I'm sure he expected me to do the same.

I wiped my hands on my shorts and didn't speak. I just wanted to keep on playing.

"He gives me a great game," said Vladie.

I jerked my head at him as if to say "Sure."

"I don't know anybody who's picked up tennis this fast," said Eric. "He's unbelievable."

"Really. No doubt."

I couldn't stand it. As far as Eric and his kiss-ass compliments were concerned, they could take a flying leap. As for Vladie, I couldn't believe how gullible he was. Couldn't he see through this kid and his paste-on smile? Eric had practically gutted Vladie in the play-off game, and now he was acting as if nothing had ever happened.

The only thing I could imagine was that everyone wanted to be Eric's friend because he was awesome on the courts. Well, I didn't give a rat's ass about how well he played tennis. He could beat THE WORLD and I wouldn't give him squat.

We finally switched sides so Eric and I were together. There was no avoiding it. I tried to stay away from him, but he came right over.

"How are the treatments going?" he asked.

I stared hard and unforgivingly at the kid. "Fine." I wasn't going to be suckered by this bastard again.

"How many more?"

I shrugged. No way, I wasn't going to let him jerk me around. I held up the ball and waved toward Vladie. "Ready?" And I served.

Eric had lost a great deal of strength from the pneumonia. He moved slower. His swing, the one I had copied just a few weeks before, was flimsy now and lacked any real power. The telling *pop* was muffled as if the ball had been wrapped in tissue paper.

Eric destroyed the rhythm of our game. He couldn't keep up. As we played, I hoped that Vladie would get a little revenge, that he would drive one right into the kid. But I knew he wouldn't. Vladie was too good for that. He had way too much class. But I could hope.

Before we got a chance to volley against Eric alone, Fredericks called us to Court One for a talk on the over-hand smash. He asked Vladie to serve up a variety of balls, and then with deadly accuracy, Fredericks slammed them home.

Eric went ape-shit, screaming, clapping his hands.

The other boys joined in, chanting, urging Fredericks to put on a show. Vladie hung up a lazy, cross-court lob just over the net. Like one of the pros on television, he crept in and pounced on the ball, smashing it to the opposite baseline.

Eric dropped to both knees and pumped one arm, "WINNER!"

Fredericks turned and pointed his racket toward him like Babe Ruth calling his shot to the outfield fence.

I turned my eyes away. It was sickening to watch Vladie, Fredericks, and the rest of the guys being taken in by this showman, this user. Things like this never made sense to me. How could they be so blind, so plain stupid? I hated this kind of ignorance. But I hated even more that Eric could manipulate somebody as old as Fredericks or as nice as Vladie. What sort of powers did he have? Why was I the only one to see through him?

When Eric began to cough, I thought that Fredericks was going to call the rescue squad. You'd think the kid was about to die right on the spot. The cough was deep, a hacking bark rippled with phlegm — it sounded so gross I thought I'd puke.

He bent over at the waist for a moment and then waved everyone off with his hand and headed straight for the locker room.

"Vladie," called Fredericks, motioning toward the group.

But Vladie had already begun to sprint to the boy's side.

The stillness of the moment was confusing, didn't fit. The kid was coughing not bleeding to death. He didn't have frigging cancer! I turned to the guy next to me. "He sure has a lot of crap in his chest. Glad he didn't spit it out on the court."

The kid wouldn't talk. He just sneered at me as if I'd kicked a little old woman or something. I couldn't figure it.

Vladie and Eric came out of the locker room a few minutes later. While the rest of us practiced over-head returns, Fredericks walked over to them, spoke for a second, and then put his hand on Eric's shoulder. He'd never done that to me.

I guess that's what really ticked me off about it all. I was the one who was really sick, and except for Barbara Allen and Eric, no one at The Racket had ever said anything to me. They knew, but they didn't seem to care. I guess I just wasn't one of them, and they weren't going to let me be either.

Fredericks called us together. "Let's play some hard points." And then he motioned toward the courts.

"You two against me," said Eric in a raspy voice.

"You up for it?" asked Vladie.

"Sure."

We began. Vladie served up a floater. *Pop.* Then back again. *Pop.* I returned a rope to the baseline, and Vladie began a commentary.

"A beautiful full volley by Brandeis to Burke's backhand. Great ground stroke. A fabulous return by Cinader. What a volley, ladies and gentlemen! An unbelievable testament to their marvelously honed skills."

"An unbelievable testament?" repeated Eric, coughing with laughter.

Vladie shrugged. "An incredible tribute?"

Eric dropped his head, then his racket.

"Staggering validation?"

"Give it up."

"An inconceivable . . . "

"STOP!" Eric sat in the middle of the court, then lay down, rolling from side to side in laughing fits laced with hacking coughs.

"Vladie at it again?" asked Fredericks. Even he was laughing after catching the last few lines.

But Eric couldn't answer.

"Vladie," chided Fredericks, "you've just got to learn how to control yourself on the court."

"Yes, Mr. Fredericks, sir. I'm sorry, sir." Vladie, smiling widely, lowered his head.

"Don't let these two corrupt you, Scott," Fredericks warned.

He didn't have to worry. The last part of practice was tie breakers. One-on-one. A chance to really get to it.

"You guys go first," said Vladie. "I got to hit the john."

"Be careful," sang Eric.

"Right." Vladie poked up his middle finger and widened his eyes.

What a fool, I thought.

I was ready for this. More than ready. I wanted to clean house on this bastard. I wanted him to suffer just as Vladie had. It was time for Eric to realize that he hadn't conned everyone.

My serve was perfect, but Eric got a racket on it and the thing dropped just out of my reach. I wasn't worried. I knew that if I could get him running that I'd suck the life out of him and bring him to his knees.

On his serve he moved right to the net, challenging me. I wouldn't bite. I dropped a lob to the baseline. He sprinted and just barely reached it.

His return was weak. I got into position quickly and dropped one just over the net. He lurched forward, but the ball bounced twice before he got a racket on it.

Now his legs were heavy and awkward. No spring. Lead posts. His time was up. I could hear his heavy breathing. See his face turning white.

On the next serve I got him moving from side to side. I loved it. I had him in my control, and I could see him straining to summon the anger that had wiped out Vladie weeks before.

I wouldn't give him the chance.

Back and forth. Back and forth.

I ran him into the ground. I could have ended it sooner, but I wouldn't.

I smothered him.

Breathless.

"Sorry." He raised his hand to surrender, then bent at the waist trying to inhale through a thick blanket of phlegm.

I leaned forward on my toes, still ready to fight. Maybe he was setting me up. Maybe he was trying to trick me and fire a shot while I wasn't looking.

But no, he was gone.

I dropped to my heels.

Game. Set. Match. Revenge couldn't have been sweeter.

* * *

That night, as I lay in bed, I saw Eric fighting his way across the court. Back and forth, back and forth. Gasping for a full breath of sweet air. I could picture his sharp eyes trying to get angry, trying to battle back. And I could see the ball landing just out of his reach. Just enough. That night, over and over again, I heard Vladie's whispered words.

"You don't know, do you?"

YOU DON'T KNOW, DO YOU?

Cystic fibrosis.

Eric had no odds.

Oh sweet Jesus, what had I done?

— 10 —

All I saw that next day was Eric. In the bathroom mirror. In the cars we passed on the ride to school. On the faces of the kids hanging out, sucking in long, deep drags of the last cigarette until morning break in the boys' room. Even my homeroom teacher's cough summoned those moments on the court with Eric, the ones that had racked my brain all night long.

Why?

The answer was all too easy. I hadn't wanted to see. I hadn't taken the time to ask. And all the signs were there. His thin body. His nasal voice. Why else would he have been so comfortable talking with me about my illness? And why else would he have thought my chances were so damned good? Why? Because I had a chance. A good chance. But his was sitting at the bottom of a test tube somewhere waiting to be discovered.

"What's up with you today?"

"Huh?"

"I said 'What's up?'"

"Nothing."

"Receiving signals from another planet? Ooooh — wee — Ooooh," he mouthed. "Earth to Scott, earth to Scott."

"Just thinking."

"Yeah, right. You've been 'just thinking' all frigging morning."

I really wanted to tell Kevin. I wanted to take him into the auditorium and tell him what I'd done to Eric. But I couldn't do it.

Kevin and I didn't get serious. There was always this wall. If I said something straight, he'd spit out something stupid. And if he tried, same thing from me. The night Coach Kiesman gave me the game ball and Kevin led me out of the gym, I never said a word. I couldn't. But Kevin had to. He couldn't let the serious stay.

"Frigging-A, man, at least they could give you a car or something."

And that's the way it always was. We didn't do serious. So, I didn't explain. I didn't want to play our game with this one.

Later that day, while Mr. Wood was lecturing about the Germans in World War II, I was back on Court Eight with Eric. It was just as clear and just as real as those moments the day before. I could hear his breathing, and I watched as his face twisted from pale white to a deep red, almost purple. It was as if I had my hands around his neck, squeezing like hell.

I had tortured him, plain and simple.

The last bell of the day rang. An explosion in the hallway as the kids charged to their lockers and raced to the buses. I didn't run. I moved slowly and took any old book out of my locker. It was a strange sensation, everyone whipping around in overdrive while I, mesmerized by the memories, wandered lifelessly through the hall.

As I weaved slowly through the crowd of kids in the lobby, I didn't see faces. I heard the lively banter but none of the words. When I stepped outside, the cool winter air knocked me out of my daze. I figured I should have gone out earlier in the day; maybe that would have helped me snap out of it.

Our car was parked out in front where it always was. My mother had a paperback novel pinned to the steering wheel. As always, she read, oblivious to the craziness spewing out of the front doors of the high school. She could read a book anywhere, at anytime.

"How was your day?" she asked bending the corner of the page as I flopped into the seat.

"Fine."

"Good."

I was surprised she hadn't caught on to the sorrow in my voice.

"Listen, I have a favor to ask," she said pointing, reminding me of my seatbelt. "I had a doubles match set for this afternoon, but Judy can't make it. Do you feel up to playing? Do you have the time?"

I didn't have to think about the answer. Anything to keep from sitting alone in my bedroom with all of those thoughts. Mrs. Cross and Mrs. MacFawn were good players. Neither of them was intimidated by my hard serve. In fact, they thrived on the challenge of a hard-hitting player, and I could tell they loved returning my tough shots. As for me, it was just the escape I needed. They were steady players who kept volleys alive for the longest times — there was no time for anything but the match.

"So, you've only been playing for a few weeks?" Mrs. Cross looked at me admiringly.

"About a month." I answered in a soft, modest voice sensing a compliment was on its way.

"I'd heard you were good, but I can't believe you're this good," she said.

"And so handsome, too," added Mrs. MacFawn.

"Wait a minute, girls," interrupted my mother. "Let's not turn this into the *Scott Cinader Hour*. I've got to live with this kid."

Both of the women laughed while I stared into the distance. I felt like a little kid again — the center of attention — and I really liked it. I don't know why, but older women always had a way with me. The slightest bit of attention and I'd turn into a shy eight-year-old all over again.

We won two out of the three sets. Afterwards, my mother and her friends went into the lounge while I volleyed against the practice wall.

The games seemed to have done the trick. I felt good again. Freed of those miserable thoughts, I felt loose. My muscles were warm and tired, and as I played against the wall, I concentrated on my strokes.

After a few minutes, I began to strike the ball more firmly. The *pop* echoed about the building. I played from side to side — deeper and farther back. Harder and harder.

My breathing joined with the *pop* and the flat, ringing rebound of the ball off the wall.

I struck it with all of my might. Sprinted from side to side. Wouldn't let up. Wouldn't rest.

Back and forth.

Back and forth.

And all of a sudden I was there again. I could see Eric's face, his eyes rolling back, his lips turned into an O trying to suck air as he leaned up against the wall and inched his way to the floor.

Hurt.

I couldn't run. Couldn't breathe.

Had to stop.

I can't.

I slipped down against the practice wall. My face burned as if little needles were piercing the skin. The sweat trickled from my chin. My chest heaved.

And still, I couldn't forgive myself.

— 11 —

Kevin and I stood side by side in the lunch line. We both wore our Red Sox hats, both had on gray sweatshirts and jeans (by accident, of course), and both took macaroni and cheese, two salads, two peanut butter cookies, and three milks.

"How come you always get the same stuff as me?"

"I want to grow up to be just like you, Scott."

"Oh yeah?"

"Yup. You're my hero. You're frigging perfect, you know?" Kevin smirked. "You're good looking, too."

"Shut up."

"No, really. You're incredible, Scott."

I gave him a dirty look. Of course, I knew it would only encourage him.

"Hey, I don't want to marry you or anything . . . I just want to be like you." Kevin batted his eyelids and smiled adorably.

"Sometimes you're too sick for your own good, you know?"

"Of course," he sang. "But that's why you like me."

I thought for a moment, looked him over, and laughed. "Probably."

"Told you." He smirked again.

"You're incredible."

"Absolutely."

"Enough," I said lifting both hands in surrender.

"Want your cookies?"

"Of course. Why do you think I took the stupid things?"

Kevin shrugged. We wolfed down our food. I threw a rotten-looking piece of lettuce onto Kevin's tray; he retaliated with a piece of slimy, over-cooked macaroni. He slipped one of the cookies off my tray – I grabbed one of his milks. Then we traded back. Another typical lunch of games. Always games. The two of us couldn't get away from them. Didn't make any difference what we were doing; it always turned into some kind of crazy contest. But at least this took my mind off of Eric.

"Betcha your cookie I can snort this tomato seed up through my nose and bring it out my mouth in fifteen seconds." Kevin's wagers always had a twisted side.

"I'll puke on you if you do."

"Where's your sense of adventure?"

"Snorting tomato seeds?"

"I'll work my way up . . . apple seeds, orange seeds . . ." he pushed his thumb and forefinger into his nostril to measure. "Maybe a baby peach stone?"

"You're sick."

"Hey, life's too short to be ordinary. So, what do you say? A quarter?"

"Kev . . ."

"Fifteen cents?"

"Shut up."

We ate in silence for a few moments both looking about the café at the different sights. A table of hard guys was giving Miss Chambliss, the new business teacher, a rough time because she asked them to take down the castle they'd made out of glass juice bottles. A table full of jocks was playing poker – there wasn't any money on the table, but everyone, even the teachers on duty, knew that the bucks were there some place. And then sitting just three tables away, Lori James and her stare. She was with a group of cheerleaders – when our eyes locked, we both looked away quickly.

As always, Kevin was fast. He was kind of like Radar O'Reilly on *M*A*S*H* – heck, he knew before I did when I had to go to the bathroom.

"So, what's up? Seen a ghost?"

"Just about."

He waited for a moment. "Yeah, well?"

"She's staring at me again," I answered, not really wanting him to know.

"Scottie, my boy," he sang. "Who's staring, you little stud muffin?"

"It's not important."

"Unh-unh. Don't do that to me. Remember, we got a deal," he said.

And we did. The deal was, if you brought a subject up, you finished it, no exceptions.

"Okay. Lori James. And before you say a stinking word, it's not what you think."

"She's in love, boy."

"No, Kevin, she's not."

"All right then, she wants your frigging body. Love. Lust. What's the difference?"

"Unh-unh."

"Listen, studly, I'm not going to sit here and feed your frigging ego all day."

"She's not interested in me," I explained, now lost for the right words.

"Why the hell would she be staring then?"

"Because."

"Ohhh . . . of course. Because. I should have known," he said dramatically throwing his hands into the air.

I fumbled for my fork and then squeezed it so hard my forearm began to hurt. I pushed the macaroni aside. Held my breath. Knew my face was flushed and that my eyes were watering. Once Kevin caught on his body stiffened and his hands went under the table and into his lap. It was the first time he had seen me cry.

"Forget her." The strain in his voice cried at me.

"It's not her."

The silence that fell between us was new. It caught us both by surprise — we couldn't look at each other, let alone speak.

It was more than Lori James now. Eric was there. Part of me wanted to crack a joke, to get away from this, to make it into a game. Part of me wanted to grab onto Kevin. Part of me wanted to run for my life.

Instead we just sat there in silence until the bell.

* * *

"I'm not going to tennis today."

My mother looked me over thoroughly. "Are you feeling okay?"

"Yes. I'm just not going."

I knew she sensed my anger and that she shouldn't try to change my mind. But as always, she had to offer. "Do you want to talk about it?"

"I just don't want to go today."

And that was it. My mother was good about stuff like this. She knew when to back off and when to give me space. We drove home without another word. I fanned the pages of my English book while she strained to keep her eyes on the road ahead. I kind of felt guilty for not being able to tell her, but then, what I had done to Eric couldn't be forgiven by her. I had to pay for it all by myself.

At home, I stared at the short story due for English. I read a couple of paragraphs, but didn't remember a word. My eyes wandered around my bedroom, from the walls to my desk, from the posters of the Celtics to a sock that lay rolled up in a ball in the corner. I looked at a picture of Kevin and me – closed my eyes and saw Eric again. Would it ever go away? I put my hands on my chest and fingered the spot where the doctor had said it was. I couldn't feel a thing – no lump, no pain, nothing.

I leaned back and closed my eyes. I summoned sleep to help me escape, to help me forget, but it wouldn't come. Downstairs I heard the doorbell ring and the front door close. Then, in a moment, the creaking of the steps leading to the second-floor. Kevin must have skipped wrestling, I thought.

A knock at my door. I rose and slowly pulled it open.

"Hi."

Eric's face loomed at me as it had in my dreams. "Hi."

"Busy?"

"Just doing some English," I said, holding up my book.

"Oh yeah? What kind of stuff?"

"Short stories."

"I love short stories."

I stood still and didn't answer.

"When you didn't show up at tennis this afternoon, I thought I'd stop by. I got your address from Barbara. I wanted to make sure you were okay."

His voice was strong and certain – I felt weak as I faced him. "I just had to get caught up on my homework." I didn't sound very convincing.

"I know how that is," he said, helping me with my lie. "I'm always behind."

I could sense my face tightening.

"You found out about me, huh? About my CF?"

I stared at my feet like a bashful two-year-old. "Vladie told me."

"It's okay, you know," he said softly. "I talked to Vladie, too. I thought because of the tie breaker we played that you might be feeling kind of crummy – as if you should have backed off or something. As if you should have known about me."

He was carefree in the way that he spoke. "Sometimes I think I should introduce myself by saying 'Hi, I'm Eric Burke and I have cystic fibrosis.' And sometimes I wish no one at all knew. Know what I mean?"

It was like some kind of dream. I couldn't believe Eric was saying all this stuff out loud. I couldn't believe he knew exactly how I felt.

"I feel bad," I blurted.

"Don't. I should have taken a break and caught my breath. I'm a big boy, but sometimes my ego gets in the way. I hate to lose," he said, grinning.

"Yeah, but I should have figured it out."

"Listen, don't be stupid. It wasn't your fault. All you did was play the game just as anyone else would have." He looked me right in the eye and smiled, "Anyway, I feel great."

Incredible. For the first time in days I could take a deep breath. "Thanks."

"Hey, no problem. Just one more thing," he said with more purpose in his voice. "I want a rematch."

— 12 —

It was no contest.

I had no idea how good Eric really was — no idea until he totally destroyed me in a three-set match. I won a point here and there, but for the most part it was all Eric Burke. His serves were untouchable. His placement nearly perfect. And when he reared back and blistered a shot down the line, forget it.

And the look was there. The fierce, vicious stare of a crazed madman being chased by hounds. Somehow, I had thought, since we had become friends that he would not turn on his savage side and attack me. But I couldn't have been more wrong. It was there. Boy, was it ever. And whenever he spoke to me, his words were flat, emotionless, as if I were a total stranger — worse yet, his enemy.

"Forty — fifteen."

"Fifteen — serving — love."

And nothing else was spoken. Not another word. I thought of cracking a joke, but no way. I remembered his match with Vladie and knew that Eric was only interested in one thing: the game. All the rest of the stuff, including the guy on the other side of the net, was incidental.

Vladie stood safely off to the side with Barbara Allen and a couple of other players from class. I knew that they were not rooting for me, and in a way neither was I. But I played with all of the energy and all of the strength that I could muster. I wanted to give him my best; that's what he deserved, nothing more, nothing less.

After the match I watched closely as Eric went through his metamorphosis, back to the old Eric, the friendly kid. It didn't happen right off, like the second he walked off the court — *bam* — a smile and his easy way. It took a while, like waking up after a long afternoon nap.

First he walked over to the water fountain and took a long drink.

Then, away from everyone else, he put on a dry shirt and his warm-up clothes. Even then, he wasn't back. The look lingered like the memory of his last ace of the match. It was a solid rope which caught the center line and duped me into lunging the other way. I looked like a baboon.

By the time he had slurped down his second drink from the water fountain and put away his racket, Eric's other side began to resurface. We sat together at the far end of the complex and watched Barbara and Vladie play a couple guys from class named Mike and Jeff.

"You can really play." I looked right into his eyes – something I rarely did.

Eric smiled. "Thank you. I've been at it for almost ten years, you know. Just think what you'll play like in ten years. You'll demolish people."

"Yeah. Right."

"Really. Just think about it. You've only played for what, forty or fifty hours? Imagine what you'll be like after a few thousand hours." His face lit up, and I could tell that he enjoyed the idea.

"I hadn't thought about it that way," I said.

Eric laughed. "Well, don't let it go to your head. You've got a lot of work to do."

I rolled my eyes. "I know. Any suggestions?"

"Your biggest weakness right now is your positioning on the court. You don't set up quickly enough – you're not anticipating. Everything else like your backhand and serves is getting pretty strong, but it's your sense of court that's not there yet."

"So what do I have to do?"

"Play."

"Yeah, of course, but – "

"Play," he repeated soundly. "You can take all the lessons in the world, watch all the videos, but none of it can replace playing. You've got to develop a feel for the game. It's like in basketball, sometimes without looking you just know where you are on the court, right?"

"Sure."

"Same thing here. And it comes from playing, from being out there hour after hour. It's got to become a part of you. Right now you've got all the right moves, but some of them have to be fine tuned. You've got to pay your dues."

I nodded and pursed my lips.

"I think you're going to be very good." The calm in Eric's voice was convincing.

"Thanks."

"Real good."

"As good as you?"

Eric lifted his eyebrows and smiled. "Probably better."

"Nah, never."

"I think so, Scott. You're stronger and quicker than I am, and you'll have more time."

My insides did a flip, and my face must have too because Eric jumped right in.

"Sorry about that. Sounds kind of morbid, huh?"

"Well, yeah."

"I didn't mean it that way."

A brief silence.

"Do you think about it a lot?" The words flowed from my lips, and I thought I sounded just like Eric.

"I think about it all the time . . ." Then, as if he were looking right through me, ". . . and never."

"What do you mean?"

"It's simple, really. This is me – this is the way it's always been. CF is a way of life. It's kind of like having a nose. You've always had one; it's no big deal. You don't really think about it, but you do. Know what I mean? So, I've always had cystic fibrosis. I don't sit around and think about it all the time just like you don't sit around and think about your nose."

"Yeah, but . . . . You make it sound so simple."

"I guess it can be as complicated or as simple as you want it to be," he said. "If I sat around and thought about things all the time, I'd go completely wacko. I probably wouldn't come out of the house."

I nodded and leaned my chin on my hands.

"And don't think I'm some kind of hero, either. I get scared, but who doesn't?" He shrugged. "Hey, the way I see it, life's like a tennis match – when you're on the court, kick some butt. When the game's over, it's over."

— 13 —

I had known from the very beginning that I would probably have to enter the hospital for intensive treatments. But somehow I held out hope that perhaps the growth in my chest would just disintegrate — that the preliminary treatments would do the trick. It didn't happen. And when the time finally arrived, I put on a good face even though I was so frightened that I always felt like crying.

The fourth floor was the children's cancer ward. When we arrived just after lunch, it was very quiet. As I was wheeled down the corridor, I glanced into the rooms. Most of the kids were pale-faced and hollow-eyed; they wore stocking caps to cover their scalps. As I looked into their faces, I remembered a black and white film we had seen in history on the Nazi death camps. I wondered how many on this floor would survive.

My room had six beds — five were filled. When the orderly rolled me in, no one looked up; no one even moved. Three boys lay fast asleep. Two younger ones, rolled onto their sides, watched television. Their ears were pasted to the remote control units in their beds.

I dreaded the thought of turning into one of these sick kids. My mother began putting away my clothes in a metal dresser while my father disappeared out the door. I could tell they were both nervous, and I had seen how they reacted as we walked the corridor and passed the rooms filled with little boys and little girls. My mother was fidgety — she folded my stuff for a second time and unwrapped my socks only to roll them up again.

"Welcome!" The shrill voice pierced the quiet of the ward. A short, stocky nurse dressed in white pants and a white top burst into the room. "I'm Mary."

"Come on, Mary. Can't a guy get a little sleep around this dump?"

complained Mark whose name, like the others, was written at the foot of his bed.

She waved him off, smiling. "Welcome to the fourth floor."

"Oh, Mary. Give us a break, will ya?" groaned Greg, another of the sleepers.

"Happens every day after lunch," explained the nurse. "The place turns into a sleep factory. Let's go, you guys. You've got a new roommate. Wake up!" she called, slapping the third boy, Don, on the foot.

"Geez, watch it!" he complained.

"They think they're tough," laughed Mary, cuffing the boy's foot again.

"You saw that, right?" Don pointed down at his foot and then at the nurse. "Let me tell you, they beat us every day."

"They're holding us against our will," added Mark.

My mother sat down next to me on my bed. Our eyes widened as the show continued.

"Yeah. And they're doing experiments on us – weird stuff like trying to make us eat four bowls of bubblegum ice cream and a family-size anchovy pizza all in one sitting."

"Honest."

"Yeah. And the other day all we could get on the TV was the education channel."

"Mr. Rogers."

"Big Bird."

"They're trying to drive us IN-SANE."

"So get out of here while you can . . ."

"Your life depends on it."

All the time the three older boys rattled on, Mary mocked them. She contorted her face and stuck out her tongue. She danced from my metal bureau over to the bathroom door while flapping her lips and waving her arms. She fit right in with the three guys.

"Whatever you do," warned Greg, "don't take the cap!" His eyes bulged out as he grabbed the top of his light blue stocking cap and pulled it off his head. His scalp, like mine, was lily white.

"Yeah," added Mark, who touched his green cap. "They're trying to clone us."

But just as Mark finished his sentence, Mary held out five caps all of different colors.

"Ahh!"

"The cap! The cap!"

"Don't take it!"

Mark, Greg, and Don held their hands and arms up to their faces as if the very sight of the caps would zap them.

"You guys have most definitely lost your minds," said Mary. "Which color, Scott?"

I took a purple one.

"That's it."

"Too bad."

"It's over," said Greg sadly, shaking his head. "They've got another one."

My mother laughed out loud. And my father, who'd caught the last few moments of chaos, smiled broadly.

"Oh, you should catch their morning act if you think this one is cute. They're in rare form after breakfast," chuckled Mary.

"I can only imagine," said my mother.

"Scott, those two kids over there are Craig and Matt," said Mary, pointing at the two younger kids.

"Aard and Vark," said Don.

"Another experiment," whispered Mark. "They're addicted to the tube."

"Especially shows about talking mice and guys who run around in colored long underwear," explained Greg.

My parents left the room sooner than I thought they ever would. I was in good hands. We knew that although the fourth floor may have been the children's cancer ward, it was also a place of life and a place of laughter.

Throughout the evening hours, the three boys lectured me on fourth floor survival tactics.

"Every day they'll ask you if you've had a 'bowel movement,'" explained Mark.

"Just say 'yes,'" urged Don.

"Really," added Greg.

"I don't get it."

"Oh, you will."

They laughed.

"No one warned me when I first got here," explained Mark, in a serious tone. "Some witch came in and asked me if I'd taken a dump that day. I hadn't, but it was no big deal. But before I could spit, she had me rolled onto my side and was driving this thing up my butt. I went. Boy, did I go."

"Same thing here," said Don, rolling onto his side and rubbing his rear.

"Not me," said Greg. "These guys warned me. I don't care if I don't go for a month, no one's going to ream me out with a rectal water pick!"

"*Roto Rooter.*"

"The thing is, some of these witches like it."

"Get off on it."

"Yup. Not Mary though."

"Nope. She's cool. But don't tell her the truth. She's okay, but she'll still flush you out if you haven't gone."

I squirmed at the thought of it. Crossed my legs and pulled the bed sheet up over my chest. *Of all things.*

Later that night one of the "witches" came by and stopped at each bed. I strained to hear, but she whispered carefully. Finally, she was at my bedside. She glanced at the chart at the end of the bed and then moved to my side. "Have you had a bowel movement today?"

I never hesitated. "Oh yes, two."

"Two?" she asked, concerned.

Holy. What have I done?

"Do you feel okay? Is your stomach upset?"

Oh no. "No, no," I said quickly. "I'm fine. I just had a big breakfast this morning. Real big."

"Okay, dear. But you let me know if you start feeling poorly."

"Absolutely."

The witch, whose name was Susan, left the ward. I could hear the muffled giggles coming from Don's bed.

"A big breakfast," laughed the boy. "You're learning, buddy. You're learning."

— 14 —

When the television was off, Craig and Matt — Aard and Vark — sounded like a couple of cartoon characters.

"Chip and Dale," said Mark as if he had read my mind.

The two kids chattered mindlessly away about everything and nothing until they drove us nuts.

"It's like if Aquaman had the powers of . . ."

"No, no. Aquaman's a fish," giggled Matt. "I'd take Superman any day."

"Superman? Nah, he's a loser. He's too into Superwoman."

Both of the boys laughed.

"I'd be Batman — neat car."

"Yeah, but he's got no powers."

"I know, but it's a great car."

"But you could have any car you wanted if you were Superman."

"Yeah, that's true."

"Really."

"I don't believe it." Mark sat up in his bed. "Listen. You be Batman. You be Superman. I'll be Wonder Woman, and we'll share the stinking car. Okay?"

The rest of us tried hard not to laugh while Aard and Vark looked at each other with bewilderment.

"Okay with you?" Aard twisted his head around and raised his eyebrows so he really looked like one of the chipmunk characters.

"Fine," quipped Vark.

The two boys nodded.

"Maybe we could have a ride in the Batmobile?" asked Don.

"Sure. No problem," said Mark.

We all laughed again. Aard and Vark looked at one another, not quite sure what to make of us and not all that interested anyway.

I felt a little guilty, for it wasn't all that long ago that I had sat in front of the TV and fantasized about being one of the Superheroes. And when Kevin and Elmer and the rest of The Tribe played in the woods near our hide-out, we all took on the powers of our favorite character. We used to race around for entire afternoons playing war and arguing about whose powers were greater.

Greg's quiet words took me by surprise. "You know what?" he asked. "I always wanted to be The Flash."

I smiled and admitted, "Spiderman."

"Okay, okay. I even had a Superman suit," said Mark. "My next-door neighbors called me the 'Red-assed Ant.'"

Matt and Craig hooted with delight and whispered "Red-assed Ant" over and over again to one another. I remembered back when I liked saying dirty words, too.

"So?" Mark looked hard at Don, waiting for his confession. "Well, Don? What was it?"

Don held his hands in the air. "I never wanted to be any of those Superhero guys," he said. "Honest."

"Sure."

"Right."

"Give me break, will ya?"

"Come on," sang Mark. "Tell us."

"Seriously," he said. "I wasn't into that kind of stuff."

"Well, what were you 'into'?" asked Mark.

Don mumbled something under his breath.

"What?"

"Dance."

"DANCE?"

"Ssssh," mouthed Don with his finger to his lips.

"What do you mean, dance?"

"Fred Astaire stuff."

"Fred Ass-who?"

Aard's and Vark's eyes lighted up again as they both mouthed the words.

"Fred Astaire. A famous dancer. He did movies and stuff."

Don sat still in his bed waiting for the jabs.

"A dancer, huh?" shrugged Mark. "Oh well."

Surprisingly, the rest of us just nodded – if he wanted to be a dancer, he wanted to be a dancer.

But as for Aard and Vark, they weren't quite that forgiving. Craig looked at Matt and leaned toward him, whispering just loud enough for all to hear, "I'd rather be Wonderwoman any day."

That evening a steady stream of visitors paraded through our room. Most of the kids' parents were upbeat and smiling; they brought energy into the room and it made me feel stronger to look at them. But Matt's parents were sad. Their faces were ashen, and they hovered around the little boy's bed as if the slightest noise or quick movement might hurt him. It made me nervous to look at them, and every time I glanced in their direction, I felt breathless and weak.

As for my folks, they struck up a conversation with Don's. They did not talk about cancer or chemotherapy, and they didn't chit chat about the weather. It just so happened that the Medds and my folks had the same cause: the State of Maine and how it was being overrun by out-of-staters.

Even our little corner store is selling *The New York Times* and brie," said Irma Medd, a big-boned woman with a fierce, low voice.

"These folks are buying up everything in sight. You name it, and it's been turned into a condo project," said my mother. "Cider mills, clothespin factories, even chicken barns – if it has four walls and a roof . . . poof, another condo."

"That's the truth," said Mr. Medd. "But we've stacked our town's planning board," he explained. "It would take a presidential decree or an act of Congress to have a condo project built in Sebago Falls. Of course, Irma's the head of the planning board," he said, with a wicked grin on his face.

"From what I gather, I suspect neither the president nor Congress would want to tangle with Irma," laughed my dad.

"Oh, you're very right," said Mr. Medd, nodding.

"Some things are worth the fight," said my mother.

"Definitely," said Mrs. Medd. "Definitely."

Don looked over at me from his bed. His eyes told the entire story. It's not that we didn't care about Maine; it was that basically we just didn't . . . care.

The sob, loud and anguished, startled everyone on the ward. Matt's mother cried out and her eyes swelled with tears. She clasped her hands and bit her knuckles as her husband put his arms around her.

"It's okay, Mommy," said little Matt. "I'm going to be okay."

I looked around the room. The other parents struggled with their emotions. Craig's folks started talking to the little boy — tried to take his attention away. But it didn't work; their voices quivered with fear as they rambled on about nothing.

Now, the room was very small, and I could not find the strength to move.

— 15 —

This new drug slithered through my veins like snakes in a pipe. I knew I wasn't supposed to be able to feel it, but I swore I could. It moved through my arms, down my chest, and into my legs — first it was warm, then it wasn't. I knew the juice was attacking the lump in my chest, poisoning it. And like the rest of the chemo I'd had, I knew it was hitting the good stuff in me too.

I shivered and fought the nausea. My entire body was one big quiver.

When they rolled me back into my room, I heard the guys.

"Don't let it get to you."

"Hang in there, Scott."

"Kick some butt."

My mother thanked them for me as I curled into a ball. I wedged my nose over the side of a kidney-shaped puke pan. The spasms erupted from deep within my stomach, down by my bellybutton. They were waves that slowly built until I felt dizzy, spinning, and then a sickening feeling hit my throat so hard I thought my whole stomach was going to come flying out.

After a while all that came up was a bitter acid. It lingered on my tongue and at the back of my throat until I found the strength to spit. My mother wiped the strings of saliva off my face with a tissue. Between the heaves, I rested and caught my breath. In a matter of moments the little tremors returned — then the waves. I tried not to make much noise.

Don and Greg had had treatments too. Listening to them vomit didn't help at all. And it didn't help Aard and Vark either, for within a couple of minutes both of the little boys let their insides fly onto the white-tiled floor. And then they cried.

The room stunk. A nurse gave us more medicine for the nausea and an orderly did the best he could with a bucket and mop. But the smell hung in the air and my father finally had to leave. Any time I was sick at home, he went into the cellar to do the laundry.

"That's the one thing your dad has a bit of a problem with," my mother said. I didn't blame him. Whenever I heard someone gagging or saw them tossing their cookies, it was only a matter of time.

As much as I knew she wanted to stay and help, I couldn't stand having my mother there. I just wanted to be alone. It was awful to look at her – the wrinkled lines of pain like incisions streaked across her face.

Finally, once the vomiting stopped, I told her to go. I'm still not sure to this day, but I think I used the F-word.

"Hey, how you doing?"

My eyes opened wider. It took a moment for them to focus, but when they did, there was Eric.

"Hey," I whispered. "How's your game?" My throat was killing me.

"It could be better," he said. "How's yours?"

"A little weak right now." My lips were dry and chapped; I could hardly move them.

"Brought you something." Eric's voice was soft. "Better than any drug."

He laid a Walkman on the bed next to my head. He attached the headphones and then inserted a tape.

"Chopin."

I must have fallen asleep because the next time I opened my eyes, Eric was gone. And if it hadn't been for the Walkman, I might not have remembered him coming.

The nausea was gone, at least for the moment, so I put on the headphones and pushed play.

It happened instantly, like the moment we pass into sleep. At first I was in western Maine climbing through the trees and up toward the rocky peak of Tumbledown Mountain. I could see the little alpine lake between the peaks of Jackson and Tumbledown. I slid my foot into the cold, spring-fed water.

It may have been a crescendo in the music or just something dancing about in my mind, but whatever it was, I moved in a flash to Court Eight.

The match was brutal. I heard the telling *pop* of the ball and racket mating. Heard my breathing – felt the short, quick strides across the court as I set up for another shot. I loved it. The rhythm – forehand, backhand, forehand, back.

And the music. A dance on the court. My legs burning. Sweat dripping from my brow.

As if I'd never had a treatment. As if I'd never been sick.

— 16 —

"I'm out of here!"

The young nurse, a substitute on the night shift, froze in her tracks. "Ah — wait. Please."

But it was too late. Suitcase in hand, *Kevin*, his head still shaved clean, stormed out of our hospital room while the rest of us tried not to give it away.

"Please," she called weakly, her eyes frantic and wide.

From the hallway he spouted, "No way. The food is the pits, and I'm bored silly."

"But you can't just leave."

Kevin looked back through the doorway with one of his innocent — looking expressions. "Why not?"

"Because," said the startled nurse.

"Oh. Okay. But I'll need a bed."

"A bed?"

"Yeah. If you want me to stay."

The young nurse scanned the room. Of course every bed had a boy. She glared down at Kevin, looked back at each of us, then cracked a smile. "You little . . . you got me."

"Yup," he said, gleaming. "Sure did."

We all looked forward to Kevin's visits, especially Craig and Matt. Even when one of us had had a treatment, it was good to listen to him tell the story of the day. We asked him to repeat some of them, like the one when he and another guy at school put clear plastic wrap beneath the toilet seats in the girls' bathroom. It was just before lunch — the busiest bathroom time of the day. "Frigging-A, man. I ain't never heard such a commotion!"

And we both told the old standbys — The Mosquito Test and The

Challenge — and had all of the guys squirming in their beds.

"Chewed up peas?" repeated Don, pulling his pillow over his face.

"You actually drank that crap?"

The other boys rolled onto their sides repulsed by Kevin's feat. They stared at him. At first I couldn't tell whether it was with respect or envy, or with total disgust. But then, the answer became clear.

The more I watched Kevin with my roommates, the more I knew why he was my best friend. The way he looked at people made me feel good. The way he listened and found just the right thing to say to make them smile. Kevin was an amazing guy.

Some days he would sit all afternoon on the edge of our beds after a treatment. If we threw up, he'd take away the pan if the nurse or our parents weren't around, hand us some Kleenex, and start talking softly as if nothing at all had happened. For me, Kevin helped take my mind off the pain for a few minutes. There was something in his voice that settled my stomach, helped me forget, and made me feel good again. In some ways he was like Chopin's music.

He was best with Matt and Craig. He brought them comic books and posters and mega-deluxe Super Hero cards with a piece of bubble gum inside that was "bigger than a buick." Once the three of them got going, it was like listening to a foreign language. Or as Don said, "Hey, Kevin can speak Chipmunk, too."

Kevin not only made us feel better, but he helped some other guys, too. Elmer just couldn't stand hospitals. "The smell," he wrote in one of his cards, "wipes me out." But lo and behold, in he walked right behind Kevin.

Elmer's face was a chalky white when he first stepped through the door of our room. He looked as if he were going to pass out right in the middle of the floor. I heard Kevin offering him a couple of words of encouragement, but when Matt and Craig saw all six-foot-six, two-hundred-fifty pounds and started chattering, Elmer relaxed.

"These must be the Chipmunks." Elmer walked between the two boys' beds and put his hands on his hips. "Which one of you pip-squeaks is into Batman?"

Matt raised his hand slowly, then giggled nervously.

"Cool. Me too."

"Really?" squeaked little Matt.

"Absolutely."

And that was it. I barely got to talk with Elmer. He sat with Kevin between Aard and Vark. Their chatter filled the room while the rest of us looked on.

Kevin had done it again.

* * *

They took little Matt out in the middle of the night. The nurses were quick and efficient. Their whispers hinted at the urgency, but because of the hour, it was more like a dream to me.

The next morning when I woke, Matt's bed was freshly made and his name plate was removed. All of his belongings, including the huge Batman poster Elmer had given him, were gone as well. Craig had an eight o'clock treatment, so did Don and Mark. None of us had a chance to talk — it was the bathroom, breakfast, and frightened quick glances at Matt's corner of the room.

I was left with the empty bed and a nurse's one — word explanation. "Acute," was all she said.

While I lay in bed with my eyes closed, I could hear Elmer and Matt. In their few days together, they'd become very close. Matt had hung on Elmer's every word. As I lay there, I could picture Matt's smile and his wide eyes staring at his big friend.

I knew what Matt had when he looked at Elmer. He felt protected, as if no one could harm him. And I knew that Matt had felt stronger and healthier with the big guy around. So did I.

I called my parents that morning and had them phone Elmer's folks. That night Kevin came alone. He stared at the sets of parents and at the clean sheets on the bed in the far corner. He settled into the chair next to me without saying a word.

The pain ripped across his face.

The next afternoon we got the news.

— 17 —

The new drug hadn't done everything Dr. Schmidt had hoped for, but, so he said, it was "a good beginning."

A good beginning.

The chemo had eaten away at my body. My muscles were flabby and my eyeballs felt as if they were being sucked into my head. At the end of the treatments, all I could think of was rest and sleeping. There were even times when the idea of death didn't seem all that bad. In fact, it was almost inviting.

I didn't really care if I went home or not. Walking hurt, so when the nurses forced me out for exercise, I wasn't exactly talkative. In fact, I was kind of a jerk. They always laughed it off, called me Mr. Grumpy, or asked if I'd gotten up on the wrong side of the bedpan.

Finally, like it or not, I got sent home. Only Don was left out of the original five in the room. The rest went home, except for Matt, and were taking treatments through the outpatient clinic. Don was to be released the next day.

"I'll give you a call," I said.

Don waved as he leaned onto his side over the puke pan.

For the first few days at home I didn't do anything but lie in front of the television on the couch. Sometimes I watched stuff, but mostly, between naps, I thought about the next round of chemo. I prayed that I wouldn't have to go back to get juiced. But, of course, I knew the odds weren't good.

As I thought about the next round, my stomach twisted. I remembered the long days in the hospital curled on my side, frightened to move for fear of getting sick again. The more I fought it, the more I tried not to think about it, the more that feeling crept up on me.

When I wasn't thinking about going back to the hospital, I mourned little Matt. I kept seeing him in his casket lying in the ground. Part of me wished I'd been able to go to his funeral. Part of me was relieved that I couldn't. Mark, Kevin, and Elmer all went. Kevin said he'd never go to a little kid's funeral again.

The night they rushed Matt out of the ward into intensive care, I woke up just in time. As they wheeled him past me, we caught eyes; at least I thought we did.

"See you later," I whispered. I don't know that he heard me. I hope that he didn't.

See you later.

"Dr. Schmidt said you've got to get moving. That you've got to get some exercise." My mother almost sounded angry.

I knew all too well that he wanted me to get back into shape so that I'd be ready for the next chemo session.

"I know, Ma. But I can't handle school right now. I can barely get around the house."

"What about coming to The Racket with me?"

I looked at her as if she'd sworn.

"Well, of course, you don't have to play," she said quickly, almost as if she'd heard what I was thinking. "You need to get out. You just need to make that first step."

I knew she was right, but I was frightened. I wanted to be healthy again, but the more I went out into the healthy world, the sicker I felt.

Deep down inside I knew I had to go, and I was glad that I did. The smell of the building was the same, a musty scent from the hot air that spewed out of the huge metal vents. The sounds were the same, too – solid *pops* resounding off the steel beams that criss-crossed above, the screech of sneakers, and the groans of people working hard.

My clothes didn't fit; they nearly slipped off me. When I looked in the hallway mirror at The Racket, I resembled a little old man. The worst part was the dark brown circles underneath my eyes – they made me look like someone who'd come out of the grave.

I stood on the edge of the courts watching my classmates volley. I saw Vladie and Eric playing hard points, moving about the court with the fierceness of tournament play. Watching them gave me strength, got my heart pounding. Psyched me up.

Barbara saw me first. She waved, called my name, and then walked quickly across the courts. The rest of my classmates stopped playing one by one and stared at me. I was wearing a coat, a scarf, and a hat, so it took them a couple of moments to figure out who I was.

"Good to see you," said Ms. Allen. She had visited me twice in the hospital, so she was used to my ghostly appearance. As for the guys who hadn't come, I knew they'd have trouble looking at my pale skin and sunken eyes.

Some of the kids came right over to my side; they never hesitated. Others approached cautiously with faint, tentative smiles. I could almost smell their fear.

That was the worst. I hated making them nervous, so I used one of Kevin's lines. "I know," I said, tossing my hands into the air. "I either look like Ichabod Crane or the Ghost of Christmas Past. What can I say?"

Everyone laughed and moved in closer. My hand was sore after shaking all of theirs. I did a good job looking them square in the eye – some couldn't look at me that way, though. Their eyes drifted as their nervous glances gave them away. I didn't blame them.

Once we'd finished with our short talk and they offered their "hang-in-there's," they moved back to their places on the court. Vladie stayed and came right up face to face with me.

"So, how you doing?"

"Well, I feel as if I've been checking headlights out on Maine Turnpike."

Vladie laughed. It was another of Kevin's lines.

"Thanks for the cards and stuff," I said. He'd sent me a half dozen tennis magazines. "Oh, no problem." Vladie spoke quietly. "I'm sorry I didn't come to visit. I just kinda thought that – well, I thought that maybe it wouldn't be a good idea. I thought it might be too crowded with family and stuff."

"It's never too crowded. If there's a next time, I hope you'll come and give the nurses some grief."

Relieved, he smiled. "Okay. No problem."

I could tell that Vladie didn't think that he knew me well enough to come visit. I wished that he had. Maybe I should have called him and invited him to come up, but that would have been really weird. I can hear it now. "Hey, you wanna come over and watch me puke?" Nope. It just didn't work.

We were still face to face. I could tell that he wanted to say something. He smiled. I smiled.

"It's really great to have you back. I'm happy that you're better."

"Thanks, Vladie."

He put his hand on my shoulder for just a moment. I knew that it was his way of giving me a hug. I patted his back in return. I almost muckled on to him, but just couldn't. Then, with a soft slap on my arm he turned and walked back to the court.

Eric had waited off to the side until everyone had said hello. I kept glancing at him – he had smiled through the whole thing.

"So, how are you feeling?"

"I've been better."

"I bet."

"How's your game?"

"I'm really on these days. Feeling tough."

"Awesome."

"So when do you think you'll be back?"

"The way I feel, probably a year or two."

"How about tomorrow?"

I looked at him waiting to see if he was going to wink or something. But he was serious.

"Hey, I'd pass out if I tried to run."

"Who said anything about running. Just come and walk around the courts a few times. Carry your racket just to get used to it."

"I can barely make it from the couch to the bathroom without my heart pounding."

"Yeah, but you've got to start somewhere. Anyway, there's not that much time."

"What do you mean 'not much time'?"

"We're in a doubles tournament in a little over three weeks," said

Eric, straight-faced.

I shook my head. "Funny."

"Seriously. Three weeks from Saturday. That gives us – let's see. Twenty-five days."

"Twenty-five days? Eric, look at me. I can barely walk. Twenty-five days, you've lost your . . . what kind of drugs are you on?"

"Well, there's an enzyme I take three times a day and an antibiotic . . ."

"Come on, you've got to be joking."

"Hey, this ain't the Olympics. If you're not up for it, we can forfeit. Or, you can bring a chair out on to the court when you're playing net. Who cares, you know. It's just that you've got to try."

"This is crazy," I said, grinning, looking toward the ceiling.

"Absolutely. So, what do you say?"

"We'll be quite the pair, partner."

— 18 —

Once I got home from The Racket, I went for my first walk. It was only around the block, slow and steady, but it was a beginning. I had to start some place.

I couldn't believe how I'd given up. How sorry I'd felt for myself. I learned a big lesson that day. Eric was a good teacher.

The next morning my alarm went off at six-thirty. I hobbled to the bathroom and took a long, hot shower. My legs were sore from the night before, but the steamy water helped soothe the muscles. As I began drying myself off, I could hear my mother and father moving about, mumbling to one another.

"Scott, are you okay?" asked my mother.

"Yes."

"Why are you up?"

"School."

I didn't hear anything, but I could sense my mother's silent cheers as she looked at my father.

"Want a ride?" he asked.

"Absolutely. I wouldn't get there until June if I walked."

They laughed.

"Pancakes?"

"Absolutely."

By the time I had dressed and eaten, I was exhausted and ached all over. I needed a nap. Really, I needed another night's sleep. But I kept seeing Eric. Kept hearing his words. And it didn't matter what I felt like; I was going to school. Besides, I could take naps in the nurse's office all day long if I wanted. The important part was being there.

At first the thought of going back to school didn't bother me at all. I'd been through just about everything, so heading back to classes didn't seem like that big a deal. But when I climbed out of the car at the front door of St. John's, my insides did flip-flops. And as my father drove away, I'd never felt quite so alone in my life.

As always, a few kids stared at me as I shuffled up the walkway. Everyone knew who I was, and everyone wanted to get a good look – without being obvious about it, of course. I knew that because I'd done the same thing myself the year before.

When Dusty Myers came back to school after his dad had died in a freak logging truck accident, I caught glimpses of him in the hallway and checked him out in the cafeteria to see if he looked any different. He didn't. The thing is only a couple of kids hung around with him. The rest of us stayed away.

None of the kids said anything as I made my way to the front door. But then what did I expect? When Dusty came back to school, I didn't say anything to him either. "Hi" would have been so simple.

The main office was crowded with kids and teachers. A young girl, a first-year student I figured, stood at the desk collecting absence notes. The boy ahead of me had a swollen face – both sides were puffed out so much that he looked like a chipmunk with a mouthful of acorns.

"Wisdom teeth," he mumbled handing her the note. She grimaced and unconsciously rubbed her own cheeks as she filled out the pass.

When I stepped up to the desk, her eyes grew wide and she looked nervously down at the note I held before her. Naturally, she knew who I was. I got the feeling that she felt stupid taking the note, my permission for having been absent.

Of course you haven't been skipping school. You're the kid who's dying of cancer.

She didn't look at the note or at me. She checked off the little boxes on the admit slip and then slid it across the top of the desk with her finger tips. She pulled her hand back quickly to make sure that she wouldn't touch me by mistake.

Wouldn't want to touch me.

But then, I would have done the same thing.

I turned with a snap. Felt dizzy. Saw white flashes. I reached my hand out for whatever I could grab – the door frame steadied me so that

I didn't end up crawling around on the floor.

"You okay?"

I breathed deeply. The white haze evaporated. I looked into Kevin's eyes. "That was weird."

"You scared me." His voice filled with concern.

"Just a head rush."

"I thought you were having the big one," he said, a little lighter now tapping his heart, rolling his eyes until they went white.

"Not this time. Definitely not in school."

We walked down the corridor to my locker. Kevin stayed right by my side, hovering, making sure I didn't wipe out on the floor. He protected me, ran interference from the kids in the hall who might run into me by mistake. Once we'd sorted out our books, we went into homeroom.

At first the kids went quiet when I walked in, but then, after a couple of "Hi's" things got back to normal. The late bell sounded just as we sat down, and Mr. Thibodeau dashed into class.

He was always late. Always carrying a ton of papers for his history classes. "Hand-out Herb," that's what the kids called him. If he wasn't standing at the copying machine in the staff room, he was writing a list of significant dates in history on the board. Herb Thibodeau had the neatest handwriting any kid had ever seen. And if any teacher was ever "into" his subject, that was Mr. T.

"Well, well," he said from the front of the class. "Scott, it's just great to have you back."

Everyone clapped. Some of the kids whistled, and I could feel my face heating up. Then, like every morning, Mrs. Arsenault blew into the microphone over the loudspeaker to test it.

Every morning it was the same thing. Two quick breaths, like a boxer jabbing at his opponent. And then the students responded with two quick breaths of their own. It was a morning ritual at St. John's, as automatic as saying the "Pledge of Allegiance." Of course, the principal knew what was happening, but it was her way of connecting with us, of showing that she had a sense of humor. Mrs. Arsenault was a pretty cool principal.

"How you feeling?" asked Kevin as the announcements sounded on in the background.

"I'm going to head to the nurse's off after homeroom. I'm already spent. I need a break."

"I'll walk you over," said Kevin.

I didn't want a babysitter, but I was kind of scared about losing it in the hallway. And besides, the way Kevin spoke, I wasn't going to have a choice.

The passing bell sounded. Mr. Thibodeau stepped to my side.

"I'm happy to see you back, Scott," he said quietly. "How are you feeling?"

"A lot better now that I'm here."

"Let me know if there's anything I can do for you," he said putting his hand on my shoulder. Mr. T. made me feel stronger.

Kevin carried my books and led me out into the corridor. The place was mobbed. Kids sprinted like maniacs, dodging open lockers and bursting through small groups of students who stood gossiping in mid-stream.

Everything seemed so crazy, so fast, and so wild that I couldn't catch up with it all. It was like a kaleidoscope with sound attached. At one point, without realizing it, I reached out and held onto Kevin's arm as two kids came racing toward us. Kevin stopped and stiff-armed the first kid right dead center in his chest.

"Slow down," he growled.

"Sor-ry," stuttered the boy glancing at me with guilty eyes. His partner stepped way wide of us to escape Kevin's reach. No one would mess with Kevin. As a wrestler, he had a reputation.

As we continued down the corridor, I tried as best I could to walk as if I were okay. But I wasn't. My legs began to wobble and my head spun. I felt as if I were going to collapse.

The nurse's office was on the first floor. When we got to the top of the stairs, I stopped and lowered my head. I knew that I wouldn't make it.

"You hold onto the handrail," said Kevin as he slipped his arm around my waist.

We must have been quite a sight going down those stairs arm in arm. I'm surprised some no-mind kid didn't come by and scream something at us. But no one did. And as weak and as awkward as I felt on the outside, having Kevin hold me up made me feel strong. I don't ever remember feeling as close to Kevin as I did when we walked down those stairs. With each step he whispered encouragement. "You got it." "That's it, buddy." With each step our friendship grew.

The hall near the nurse's office was empty. I stopped and steadied myself on the water cooler. Beads of sweat appeared over my upper lip and I could feel my face tingling. It was as if I'd been running some of Coach Kiesman's Death Sprints.

As I took the last few steps to the office, the world whipped by in splashes of color – like being caught up in a huge blender.

And like a tight-rope walker, I didn't look down or to either side. I placed one foot in front of the other and steadied myself on my friend.

A loud sound caved in my ears and invaded my entire body like a mammoth crashing wave.

I snapped awake.

Body stiff.

Lost.

Frightened.

My name?

Stood dizzily. Waved my arms about as if I had no control over them. Swallowed. Blinked. Rubbed my face.

Where am I?

What time?

I sat back on the bed and looked about the room. Bit by bit pieces came to me. But the loud buzzer ripped at my ears, plowed deep into my head like a non-stop volley of big guns.

Or was the game over?

Did we win? Go home.

I pushed the door. Wandered into the open.

I couldn't find the controls.

Half time? The voice was soft. I trusted it. Moved to it. The voice drowned out the buzzer – grounded me. Gave me direction. Took me by the hand down the hallway.

Things cleared. Morning at school. A nap.

The fire alarm.

Now through the door. A rush of cold Maine air. Late winter.

I was back.

But this hand? This voice?

Lori James.

— 19 —

That night I fell asleep immediately. Sound. Deep. Never dreamt. The kind of sleep that's more like death.

When my alarm went off at six-thirty, I rolled over and shut it off without the slightest thought of school. And then I was gone again. A still, quiet sleep.

By nine-thirty the sun began shining through the cracks in the window shades of my room. The morning light warmed my face and tapped at my eyelids until I unraveled myself from bed. My body felt as if it were in the midst of a huge yawn – my muscles stretched, a soft ache drifted through my arms and legs. I was wide awake with clear thoughts in a matter of seconds.

As sore as I was from walking around school, I felt incredible, as if I'd been playing back-to-back, full-court games for a whole day. A sweet ache.

I was glad that my mother hadn't awakened me. I knew the extra sleep had done me good – it was a lot better than the nurse's office. Anything was better than that cot.

And then, of course, there was Lori James. *Holy.* What a mistake I'd made. If my mother had said it once, she had said it a million times: "Don't make quick judgments." And boy, in this case I'd made a corker.

The morning before when I snapped awake to the fire alarm and wandered around the hallway in a stupor, Lori came to my rescue. At first, I was way too out of it to realize, but once I had stepped outside into the winter air, my mind cleared.

And there she was. Lori James, the girl who had seemed so frightened of me. Now she was my guide, and when I looked down at my hand in hers, I really wondered if I was awake. It was like stepping up in the darkness expecting to hit the next stair, but there's nothing. You fall forward in the emptiness, startled, frightened, and for the briefest moment you wonder where your foot will land . . . or if it will.

As she led me across the parking lot, I figured that she would leave me when the fire drill ended. But it didn't happen. Her soft voice had no fear in it at all, and she held my hand firmly. The strength of her grip gave me confidence and a kind of courage.

Later, back in the nurse's office, we sat on the cot and spoke quietly to one another.

"How are you feeling?" she asked, her eyes as warm as her voice.

"I'm okay. I think I could have used a longer nap though."

"Oh, I bet. My brother was always taking naps. I kidded him about it all the time."

I looked at her and asked with my eyes.

"He had cancer, too." She looked down and I knew that she was picturing her brother. She didn't seem upset; in fact, her face glowed once she had mentioned his name.

Somehow I knew that her brother had died. She didn't say so, and I didn't ask. I really didn't have to. But now, knowing the other side, everything became much clearer.

She pushed my shoulder playfully and began to laugh. "You know, you looked like a zombie in the hallway."

"I felt like one, too," I laughed. "As if I were on some kind of cheap drug – *bzzzzz*," I sounded, waving my arms like I was playing airplanes.

"I've woken up like that, not knowing where I was or what I was supposed to be doing. It's crazy. Scary, too."

"It is."

Lori straightened out my baseball cap as we sat for a few moments in silence. It wasn't an uncomfortable quiet. We smiled back and forth a couple of times, and I knew that I'd remember this day for a long time to come. I always marked those times when I met someone new. And I could remember all of the firsts in my life – the first kiss, the first dance, the first time my hand "accidentally" brushed against a girl's breast and the tremor that invaded my whole body. That was the best first of all.

It was Lori who finally broke the quiet that morning. I could tell she wanted me to know that she understood, that it was okay. But mostly, she wanted me to know that she'd been there before.

"My parents didn't tell me right off about my brother, Ian. They didn't think I should know how sick he was. They didn't think I could handle it."

I could see by her sharp eyes that the anger and hurt were still there to a small degree.

"I knew from the very beginning. And I could handle it. He was my brother."

I nodded. "Parents do stupid things sometimes. I always thought they had all the answers. That they were perfect. But now I know."

Lori tightened her lips for a moment, thinking. "When Ian died . . ." she glanced up to see my reaction – I didn't flinch, ". . . my parents didn't know how to tell me. I had to say it to them."

I couldn't believe how open she had been or how strong she sounded. Lori was nothing like the girl I'd imagined at the library table. That day she looked as if she were frightened to death and couldn't find the strength to look me in the eye. I had been so wrong.

"You remind me of Ian," she said.

"I look like him?"

She laughed softly. "No, not at all. It's just something in your eyes." She lightly touched the brim of my baseball cap; a shiver raced up my back and left me breathless.

I knew what she was talking about. My friends on the fourth floor had it. Eric did too.

We all shared the same secret.

The phone rang.

"Hello."

"Scott?"

"Kevin?"

"Who else?"

"What's up?"

"You alive?" asked Kevin.

"No," I said dryly.

"Oh. I was just checking. See ya."

"Kiss what?"

"Yeah. Right. Anyway, guess what?"

"Not having been informed to the highest degree of accuracy I find a deficiency in articulating for fear of deviating from the true path of rectitude." One of The Tribe's best.

"Holy," said Kevin in disgust.

I laughed. "What?"

"What what?"

"You said 'Guess what?'"

"Oh, yeah. Guess what?"

"Not having been informed to . . . "

"Holy. Shut up. This is serious. Guess who asked about you today in school?"

I smiled, waited for a couple of seconds, and then whispered, "Lori James."

Not a sound.

Finally. "You know, sometimes you really . . ." Silence.

In a moment I heard a snicker.

— 20 —

My goal was to walk ten times around the courts at The Racket. I had decided that it would be good for my arm to carry my racket and practice swinging, and good for my mind to study my classmates' play — especially Eric's. Watching my friends play would help me get back into it. I knew one thing for sure; I wasn't going to be playing tennis that night.

Both Jack Fredericks and Barbara Allen were teaching class that evening. I overheard Vladie and one of the other kids saying that the teachers were "seeing each other." I couldn't think of a more unlikely pair — he so strict and cold, and she engaging and warm. It just didn't make any sense to me.

As I walked around the outside of the courts, I felt comfortable. In school the day before there was no order — kids sprinting around the hallways, teachers dishing out crazy assignments that didn't connect, and everyone racing, talking at once. Being in school had made me nervous. I felt like a stranger. But here, there was order. Sides and rules. A rhythm and a pattern. Like home.

I loved the different smells, too: sweat, sneakers burning across the floor, new tennis balls. In the hospital all the smells were wrapped in the same sterile scent like washed-out Clorox. Even the food smelled the same, and it tasted like flavored cardboard.

It was good to see healthy people again. Kids sprinting. Muscles straining. Sweat darkening the backs of shirts and shorts. My heart pounded as I watched Vladie and Eric volley, a friendly battle of strength and nerve and confidence.

"Nice get."

"Fifteen — serving — love." I loved the sounds of tennis, too.

During those moments of walking, I felt and saw more than I could ever remember. It was as if all my senses had been turned off while in the hospital, and then, with the flick of a switch, they were lit up, tuning in everything around me. As crazy as it sounds, I felt as if I had come back from the dead.

Fredericks stopped the players for a few minutes and gave a tactical lecture on net play. Afterwards, they divided up for doubles. There was an odd number, and Vladie's group had an extra player.

"Odd man out does laps with Scott," announced Vladie. "I'm first."

I thought it was cool that Vladie had thought of me and had insisted that he be the first to join in my workout.

"Want some company?"

"Absolutely," I said. "I was just about ready to start talking to myself."

Vladie chuckled. "I bet."

"So, are you entering the tournament?"

"Yup. Me and Ms. Allen are going to be in the mixed doubles."

"Wow, you guys ought to clean up!"

"I don't know about that. There are some incredible mixed doubles partners. Mr. Fredericks and Kathy Bragdon have entered. And then I know of at least three teams of married couples that are big hitters. It's not going to be an automatic, that's for sure."

"Still, it'll be awesome to play with Ms. Allen."

"No doubt."

"Anyway, all you can do is what you can do."

Vladie laughed. "Pretty philosophic."

"Yeah. Comes from eating hospital food."

We walked slowly around the courts. It seemed so slow that I felt as if I would drive Vladie crazy.

"So what do you think about Allen and Fredericks?"

I searched for a witty response. "I can't see it. Game. Set. But no match."

Vladie brushed my shoulder with an approving hand. "I know. I can't see it either."

"They'd have some pretty hot kids on the court, though."

"Yeah, but can you see the two of them . . ."

Vladie laughed. "No way."

As we moved close to the water cooler, I pulled up and took a long, slow drink. At one point I dropped my head beside the cooler and drew in a deep breath — I was actually winded from the laps. I smiled to myself, half in disgust and half in amusement. *Walking*, I thought.

We didn't talk during the next lap. I figured Vladie thought that I needed a rest. But that wasn't it.

"Well?" Eric jogged to our sides.

Vladie looked helpless.

"Oh for pete's sake, just ask him. It's no big deal," said Eric. "He's a big boy."

"Ask me what?"

"My mom's a health teacher at Portland High, you know," blurted Vladie looking at Eric in disgust.

I had known that.

"Go on," urged Eric.

"Come off it," snapped Vladie.

"Are you guys going to punch it out?" I asked.

"No," said Eric. "Sorry, Vladimir. I just didn't think it was that big a deal."

"Yeah. Well, it isn't," said Vladie, sounding a bit peeved with himself. "Sorry. My mother was wondering if you'd come in and talk with her classes."

"Me? About what?" The second I saw Vladie's eyes look down I knew exactly.

"Oh, you mean about having cancer."

"Exactly," said Eric. "I've been going in and talking for the last couple of years about CF — we could go in together."

"I'm not sure what I'd say."

"They'll ask questions. Mrs. Brandeis has them all primed," said Eric, sounding like an old pro.

"You mean about chemo and stuff like that?"

"Exactly."

The thought of standing up in front of a bunch of kids that I didn't know gave me butterflies. Actually, it scared the hell out of me.

"You don't have to tell me now," said Vladie. "Just think about it."

Think about it? I was sure I would.

Eric turned to Vladie. "Your turn to play. I'll walk with Scott."

"I don't think I could do that," I said as we made our way around the courts.

"I've got to tell you, it's pretty cool."

"Why?"

"Well, first thing is that Mrs. Brandeis is incredible. The kids are wicked polite. They ask good questions and really listen when I talk. I feel as if I'm doing something important."

"It reminds me of when I was in grade school and this man gave an assembly," I explained. "He had smoked cigarettes his whole life and got throat cancer."

As we walked I could hear this man's voice. "He had a white patch of cloth on his neck and he kind of burped to get his words out. It was really weird. Gross, too."

Eric stopped and listened carefully.

"At the end of his talk about how bad cigarettes were, he lifted up the cloth and showed us this hole in his throat. A lot of kids screamed and turned their eyes. Some kids even cried. As we went back to our classes, a couple of kids started mimicking the man – you know, burping and talking. Then a bunch started telling jokes about him, wondering whether he put his cigarette inside of his hole and sucked in."

Eric had a sad look on his face as I told the story.

"By the end of the day we were all burping as we talked. Everyone laughed at the guy. All of us."

I could hear the gritty-sounding words that I belched out back then. I had the strangest feeling that I was going to start talking that way right in front of Eric. Now, I was embarrassed at the way I had treated the man. Maybe this was some kind of payback?

"We had some of those scare tactics when I was in elementary school, too. It didn't work. I could have cared less," admitted Eric. "Talking to Mrs. Brandeis' class is different. A lot different."

He turned and we started walking again.

I couldn't picture Eric with me and my friends in elementary school laughing at the man with the hole in his throat. It just didn't fit.

— 21 —

Mrs. James had one of those smiles that grabbed right hold of me. I liked her immediately. I could feel her strength, and in a lot of ways she reminded me of my mother and the other mothers on the fourth floor. All of them had a way, a certain dignity, a grace, and a powerful presence that radiated from their eyes.

"So, how are your treatments going?" she asked without hesitation, a seasoned veteran of chemo.

"I just finished a series," I answered.

"They're good people on the fourth floor, aren't they?"

"Absolutely," I said, never having thought about her son, Ian, and the fourth floor. But of course, where else?

"We still go back to visit with the nurses and to give platelets," she said. "Some people think it's a bit strange to go back and visit, but — "

"I don't think it's strange," I interrupted. "Some people don't understand."

"You're right. They don't." The fourth floor mother came out in her with a vengeance. "Our time on the fourth floor was important." Her eyes became distant as she looked beyond both Lori and me.

I could tell that Mrs. James had been a strong cancer mother. That she gave other folks strength as they struggled to face their children's illnesses. And I knew that she did everything possible for her son, just as my mother was doing for me.

As she stood in their kitchen, I could tell that she wasn't angry about losing Ian. I knew that she was sad and that part of her heart had been taken away, but I sensed that she had worked things out. Now as she faced me and all of those reminders, I had the feeling that somewhere in the back of her mind she was enjoying a private memory of her son.

Lori and I went up to her room to listen to music. Mrs. James went off in the other direction, announcing, "I guess I'll clean the bathroom. It's my therapy, Scott."

"And boy, do we have a clean bathroom," joked Lori.

Mrs. James waved the cleaning liquid and sponge above her head as she strode off down the hallway.

While Lori flipped through her tapes and CD's, I checked out her room. She had a ton of posters pinned up on her walls and ceiling – everything from rock groups to a wild-haired Einstein. There were photo albums, a half dozen or more, and dozens of little knickknacks all over the place. On her bureau was a collection of pictures, the largest of which showed Lori standing arm in arm with a handsome, fair-haired boy.

She turned up the volume by degrees. Rolling Stones. I sat back on her bed leaning on my elbows and looking up at the posters on the ceiling.

"Loud enough?" she asked. I nodded.

Lori sat next to me, brought her knees up to her chin and cradled them in her arms. Her eyes were closed and she gently rocked to the music.

Directly above her bed was a poster of five kids standing side by side – one of the kids was Lori. It was one of those posters made from a photograph. There were three girls, one boy, and then one kid that I couldn't exactly tell. All of them wore baggy, over-sized sweatshirts and baseball caps as if they were a uniform.

"That's you in that poster, isn't it?" I asked, pointing toward the ceiling.

"Yes. That's Ian and me. My cousins, Kimberly and Tanya. And the last one is Spitter."

"Spitter?"

"He spit a lot."

"I wasn't sure whether he was a boy or a girl."

Lori laughed. "That's him. No one could ever tell when he was little. You could now, though. He's huge."

"It's a great picture," I said, squinting to inspect Spitter's face.

"Our parents called us the 'Rat Pack,'" she said.

"The Rat Pack?"

"Yes. But we had our own name."

"Oh yeah, what was that?"

"I can't possibly tell you that," she said playfully. "It's a secret. Club rule."

"Oh come on," I whined like a nine-year-old.

"No way. I'd be out of the club."

"I'll tell you about my club. We called it The Brotherhood of the Tribe," I said without hesitating.

"The Brotherhood of the Tribe?"

"Yup. The Tribe for short. Best club in Maine."

Lori looked up at the ceiling and smiled. Her eyes sparkled as she took in the picture.

"Well?" I urged. "I told you."

"I told you," she mimicked.

"Oh come on."

"Okay. But you can't tell anyone," she said making a cross over her heart.

"I promise."

We were like a couple of little kids, so far removed from the reality of my illness and the death of her brother that it was almost bizarre. But I knew that it was healthy – that sometimes, as Kevin always said, "You've just got to blow it off." And that's what we were doing.

She smiled broadly, looked around the room as if someone might be listening in, and whispered, "The James Gang."

"Ha! Great."

"We had such a good time at our cottage on the lake. We used to spy on the people down the road. Peek into their windows at night. They were never doing anything but reading, but it was the idea of it. We put on plays for all the neighbors – stuff we wrote. We wore the craziest costumes; everyone came and laughed until they hurt. And then we had a restaurant."

"A restaurant?"

"Yes. We went to all the neighbors around our cottage and borrowed food. Then we'd make up a menu with all kinds of different stuff and invite everyone to the opening. We made pretty good money."

"You sold them their own food?"

"Well, we prepared it," snapped Lori indignantly. "It was good, too."

"I'll bet."

"Seriously."

I put my hand over my mouth.

"Don't be a rat," she said trying to be serious. "Anyway, what do you know?"

"Hey, I was in a club, too, remember."

"The Brotherhood of the Tribe. What kind of club was that?"

"Tougher than yours."

"Hmmm!" she grunted.

"I'd like to see you survive The Mosquito Test."

"The Mosquito Test, huh?" She looked at me skeptically, yet didn't ask.

I played along for a few moments, but ultimately couldn't take it. "Well?"

"Well what?"

I stared at her and refused to say anything else.

Finally, she asked. "Okay. All right. What's this bug test?"

I smiled. "I can't tell you."

"You rotten . . ."

"I'm only kidding. Don't blow a gasket."

She plopped a pillow over my head.

"Okay. Here's how it went. Guys who wanted to join The Tribe had to go out into the woods near the swamp and sit in their underwear while the mosquitoes ate them alive. They had to sit still for ten minutes without slapping."

Lori squirmed and rubbed her arms as if she were being attacked by swarms of mosquitoes.

"I told you it was tough."

"It's stupid."

"It is not."

"Is too."

It felt good to laugh and to act foolish – to argue over nothing.

Lori pulled my baseball cap down over my face, and I fell forward into her arms. I could feel her tense up for an instant, but then, her arm moved onto my shoulder. We sat there, shyly silent and still, until the album finished.

"The Test is tough," I said gently.

"Is not," she whispered, slapping the brim of my hat as she stood to switch the music.

"Lori?" A deep voice called outside her bedroom door and startled both of us.

"Hi, Dad."

The door opened. Mr. James, a tall, rugged man stepped in. He wore a dark gray, three-piece business suit and looked every bit like a banker.

"Hi, Honey. Where's your mother?" he said kissing her on the forehead then glancing toward me.

"The bathroom. Dad, this is Scott Cinader."

"Hi, Scott. I'm Ian James."

My throat tightened as I heard his name. And then I saw the smile on his face disintegrate as we shook hands and he got a closer look at me.

He knew. Stepped back. His face contorted with that look of fear. I knew the memories ripped at him.

"Got to get out of this outfit," he said quickly, retreating through the door without looking at me again. "See ya, Dad." Lori hadn't caught all of this because she was fiddling with the stereo.

I couldn't blame him, really. My bald head and pale skin had to have triggered the pain of his son's death.

The music began.

I wanted to start kidding again with Lori. I wanted to fall back into her arms.

The poster. Back to the poster and the clubs.

"Boy," I said, "you and Ian really look alike."

"Twins" was all I heard.

The music blared.

* * *

As I lay in bed that night, faces and voices floated above me. I saw Mr. James — and his eyes. I wondered whether he would ever be the same. If he would ever be able to stop the pain from resurfacing. Did his stomach twist and hurt like mine? And I wondered how often he thought about his son. Every day? Most certainly. Every hour? Probably. Every single minute of every single day?

I pulled the sheet and blankets over my head. Rolled onto my side and tried to clear my head. Sleep was all I wanted. I pictured myself taking foul shots. One. Two. Three. Strained to hear the snap and *swish* of the net.

But then I rolled back. Landed with my head propped up on the pillow. Stared into the pitch dark of my room.

Back to my coffin. Shiny, sleek mahogany.

Dark blue suit.

Hands crossed.

Dead still.

My friends filing by, staring.

No!

I sat up. Reached for the light next to my bed and snapped it on.

I could study for biology. Read some English. Leaf through back issues of *Sports Illustrated.*

I could do anything, but I wasn't going to die again in that bed.

— 22 —

The corridors in school were a zoo this Friday morning. Bright blue skies and warm weather screamed the coming of spring. We could barely contain ourselves — I wondered how the teachers felt. Did they want to be stuck inside? Did they really like cinder block walls and chalk dust? Probably.

Kevin and I tripped through the hallways slapping our friends playfully, cracking stupid jokes, and whispering crude comments to one another about some of the better looking girls. Spring fever in Maine — there was nothing like it.

Kevin had just gotten a fresh hair cut — another buzz job. We were both wearing our Red Sox caps.

"You know, you don't have to keep getting your hair shaved off."

Kevin shrugged as he stopped at a water cooler for a quick slurp.

"Really," I insisted.

"I know." He turned his head away from the cooler and a dribble of water ran down his chin. "But you know what?" he asked, wiping his chin with the back of his hand. "Honestly?" He gave me one of his looks — eyebrows up, tilt of the head, shrug of the shoulders. "I like it. I really do."

Off we went without another word. He'd been as convincing as Kevin could be with his high-pitched, careless "I like it." But the farther we went down the hall, the more it didn't wash. I grabbed onto his cap and tugged it over his eyes. Without getting all stupid and sentimental on a beautiful spring-like day, this was the only way I could say thanks.

As we arrived at biology class, I saw Lori stooped over rummaging through her locker.

"Lose something?" I asked.

She turned slightly. "Hi. My history notebook."

"Nice buns," whispered Kevin just loud enough for both Lori and me to hear.

"Kevin . . ." I glared at him. Couldn't believe he had said it. But Lori didn't flinch. She found her notebook beneath a pile of books at the bottom of her locker. She stood, expressionless, looking at the two of us.

"Was he in your club?" She pointed at Kevin as if at a squished toad in the middle of the road.

I nodded, praying that she wouldn't hate me because of him.

"Must have sat on that log too long. Mosquitoes drained his brain." With that, she shut her locker, smiled at me, totally blew off Kevin, and strode down the hallway.

"You told her about the test?" asked Kevin.

I laughed.

"How could you tell her? It's a secret."

"She slammed you!"

For a moment Kevin tried to act as if he hadn't heard. But he couldn't hold on. His face cracked into a classic Kevin grin. "She sure did. She dropped me like yesterday's garbage," he said. "She sure is something."

"Sure is," I said under my breath as we walked into class.

Mr. Waite passed back our unit exams. We looked them over and then, as always, quizzed anyone within earshot about their grade. There were the usual moans and threats of suicide. Most of the kids who did well didn't say much. There were already reading the next chapter and taking notes.

"You got an 83?"

"My old man's going to kill me."

"Sweet, merciful . . . "

"A 70! I passed. I didn't even cheat."

Mr. Waite moved among us quickly, answering questions, congratulating some with a pat on the back and encouraging others with a whispered word. I knew we were his favorite class — I could just tell. It was the kind of class where we didn't always talk about the subject. We got our work done, but there was always time for personal stuff, too. Even Mr. Waite shared. Once, when he'd been out of school for a week, he told us about his brother's bad heart attack and how he'd stayed with him in intensive care for three days straight. He hadn't told any of his other classes. I had the feeling that even some of the teachers didn't know. But he'd told us.

"If you'd like to earn an extra five points, the option to write an outside report is always there," he announced.

"What's the chances of doing four or five of them reports?" asked Jarod.

"Slim to none," cracked Mr. Waite.

"I know, I know, and Slim's out to lunch," groaned the boy. "Just checking. It was nice knowing you all. This is the end. My mother's going to gut me with an old kitchen knife." Jarod slipped down over his chair until his head disappeared beneath the desk.

Normally, for me, an 86 would have sent me into orbit. Science had never been my best subject, even though I usually landed a high C or a low B. But now, with as much time as I had to study, I expected more. And not only that, I just felt that I should do better. That I had a greater obligation to do well. That I owed it to someone. To my parents? To myself, maybe.

I looked over at Kevin. "What'd you get?"

"A 73," he said proudly, holding the paper up so that I could see the big red "D" next to the 73.

"All right."

"You?"

I told him.

"What? Are you turning into a brain or something? Gonna be a doctor?"

"No, I just studied."

"Holy. I studied, too."

"How long?"

"At least an hour," he said, rolling his eyes as he thought. "Yeah. An hour. I remember because I was watching *The NBA Today*. That's an hour show."

"Yup. You're right. One hour." I wasn't going to lecture Kevin on his study habits. Who was I to talk? Anyway, he would do fine. He always did. "I ain't the brightest bulb in the circuit, but I ain't no drooler either."

That was Kevin. He did what he did, and no amount of prodding, encouraging, or ridiculing was going to change him. "Can't make chicken soup out of chicken shit," he'd say.

Nope. Can't.

While everyone talked about the test, Mr. Waite stood at the chalkboard writing furiously. He scribbled a revised list of chapters that we would read for the remainder of the year. With all my extra time and out of sheer boredom at home, I had paged through some of the sections that we were going to cover in the biology book. Chapter twenty-three was on diseases, and a good part of that was on cancer.

There was no chapter twenty-three on the board when Mr. Waite put down the chalk.

Once the class had ended, I remained seated at my desk. I wanted to say something to Mr. Waite; I wanted to tell him that if he was changing the list on my account, well, not to worry. Unlike speaking to Mrs. Brandeis' class — which I hadn't decided on yet — talking about cancer in my own school seemed okay; in fact, maybe it would help some of the kids who felt uncomfortable around me. I had the feeling it would be good for me, too. In all my weeks at school since being diagnosed, I'd never spoken about it in any class. Not once.

Before I had a chance to say something, Mr. Waite, head locked straight ahead and eyes focused on the door, escaped from the room.

As I sat there, I began to wonder. Was he worried about my feelings, my classmates', or his own?

— 23 —

"You playing tonight?" asked Vladie.

"I think so."

After walking for a week, my legs were beginning to come back. I could see the muscles in my thighs and could even jog a bit. My arms and upper body weren't quite as strong as my legs, but I felt as if I could play. Actually, I knew it was time.

"Want to volley?" asked Vladie.

"I'm going to stretch for a while." And that was true, but I was also looking for Eric. For a lot of reasons I wanted to play with him first. It just seemed like the right thing; after all, we were partners.

As I lay on the floor and watched my friends volley back and forth, I kept a sharp eye out for Eric. My legs felt extra strong this afternoon and I was anxious to get to it. After a few moments I thought that maybe I'd just start playing and forget about stretching and Eric, but just as quickly I knew what was right. Patience. No sense ending up injured after all this time, but mostly, I wanted to wait for my friend.

I stood and gently lifted my foot back into my butt stretching the quad of my right leg as I leaned forward. I admired the definition of my muscles as I flexed. It made me feel healthier to see that they were coming back. For as long as I could remember, I had thought that my upper leg muscles were the most perfect part of my body. Of course, I'd never tell anybody that, except maybe Kevin as we compared our legs. Anyway, people could see for themselves.

Once I'd finished stretching, I took a couple of walking-jogging laps around the complex. My heart pounded as I jogged. I took deep breaths — my lungs ached, but I loved the feeling.

"You're looking pretty fit today," said Ms. Allen jogging to my side.

"Not up for a marathon."

"Vladie said you're going to play a bit."

"I think I'm ready." I glanced back toward the entrance.

"Eric's mother called. He's not coming tonight," she said.

I know my face said it all.

"A friend of his is in the hospital," she said immediately. "He's visiting."

"Oh."

"I guess it's serious. His friend has CF, too."

I lowered my eyes. Felt that pain.

I'm sure that Ms. Allen sensed how I felt. "Would you like to hit around with me?"

"I don't know how long I'll last," I admitted. "Won't be much fun for you."

"Not much fun? I'd love to play with you," she said warmly, reaching out and touching my arm.

We took Court Eight. While I stood on my side of the court, I could feel a tightness in my stomach. I wondered how much I had lost. Whether it'd be like starting all over again. But even after the first stroke, things began to click.

I didn't have any power in my swing, but the ball went exactly where I wanted most of the time. It was as if I'd willed it there. Our first volley lasted for almost a minute. Back and forth. Firm hits. Lobs. Cross-courts. I loved the feeling and the rhythm. As I played that first volley, I sensed that something was weird, that something was different. When the ball skidded past me to end our first series, I knew exactly what it was. Our rackets and our footsteps were the only sounds on the courts. The whole class had stopped to watch us play.

"Great stuff!" Vladie shouted and whistled.

And all the other players clapped and cheered. Ms. Allen fought back the tears as she, too, began to clap. Even the guy at the main desk had stepped out and joined in. I raised my racket slightly, embarrassed with the attention, and walked to the back of the court.

I gained strength with each swing and lost myself in the playing. The aches and pains in my arms and legs disappeared. I focused on the ball floating across the net. Heard the solid *pop* of the racket. Felt the sweat beading on my forehead, running into my eyes, streaking into the corner of my mouth. It was not the sweat of sickness, nor a sweat brought on by the juice. It was the sweat of an athlete working hard, knowing, seeing, straining for the point. I loved that feeling.

The clock on the wall showed that I had lasted for about fifteen minutes; it had seemed longer to me. Light-headed but happy, I walked to the water fountain. I felt as if I had played for hours and that I'd been in the biggest game of my life.

"Looks as if you'll be ready for the tournament." Vladie leaned against the wall at the fountain. "Think you guys will win?"

I laughed. "I'm so far away from being fit that it's crazy. I just want to be in the thing. Look at me. There's no way we can win." I held my arms out to my sides so Vladie could take another look at my withered body.

"You never know," he said seriously.

I smiled at him and at his generous words.

It was great to be back.

— 24 —

I couldn't wait to get to The Racket the next afternoon. All I could talk about in school was playing tennis. I drove Kevin crazy.

"Listen, enough with the ultra-badminton talk. Okay?"

But I knew he was happy for me, and he had even hinted at getting a lesson himself. "Okay, Scottie. Get me one of those racket things, show me how to hold it, and I'll kick your ever-loving butt all over the place."

That afternoon when I walked into The Racket, I looked immediately toward Court Eight for Eric. Sure enough, he was on his back, Walkman at his side, stretching.

As I drew closer, I saw that his eyes were closed. I sat down near him and could hear the music spilling out of his headphones. The music had a tinny sound, but there was no doubt what it was. I pulled out the extra earphones, carefully plugged them in, and lay back. He never budged.

There was something about the music and the way Eric lay so still and quiet that settled me down. All day I had been wired to play, but once I heard the piano, I relaxed.

The music took me immediately. It could have been that I was tired from school; this day was the first that I hadn't taken a nap in the nurse's office. Or it might have been that I was just plain old exhausted from fantasizing about my game. All day long I had volleyed in my mind — had played "winners" to the baseline and smashed overhead after overhead to the feet of my faceless opponents. Whatever, I left the court and drifted off. In time, Eric stirred and poked me in the shoulder. I'm not sure where I was, but I do know it was a peaceful place.

"Chopin is a master."

"Absolutely," I said, stretching my arms out above me.

As we sat, I wanted to ask about his friend. My stomach twisted as I tried to think of the right words. It was always the same thing. How could I phrase it? Would I sound nosy? Would I hurt his feelings?

It came to me in an instant, as if someone had waved a wand above my head or whispered in my ear. I was more worried about myself and my own feelings than I was about his. I was more concerned with how uncomfortable I would be. It was the way some of the kids in school had treated me, and here I was doing the same thing to Eric.

"How is your friend?"

Eric smiled and said not good. Then, he told me their story.

Brian and Eric had known each other since they were nine years old when they met at a summer camp for kids with CF. It was the first time that either of the boys had been away from home. The first time they'd had someone other than their mother or father take care of them (except for when they were in the hospital). And even though they were two of the healthier kids at camp, both of them were miserably homesick.

The counselor's name was Doug. A six-foot-four football player from Boston University, Doug Whiting had worked at the camp for five years, ever since his kid brother had died from CF. Everyone loved Doug. He could coax a smile out of any kid, and this was why the head counselor had called on him to work some magic with Brian and Eric. They both had wanted out after the second day of camp; in fact, Brian had packed his suitcase.

The boys didn't know each other, but they both knew Doug. Everyone at camp knew him. They'd seen his lakeside antics, tripping off the end of the dock, belly flopping from the diving board. But most of all, like everyone else at camp, Brian and Eric had loved to watch Doug water ski.

From what Eric said, it was tradition that Doug water ski at the opening-night ceremonies. The other counselors went through the annual ritual of persuading their enormous friend to ski. Then, fully clothed, and after a lot of pleading and prodding, he swaggered onto the dock. He only removed his shoes and socks. The place went crazy.

I could tell from the sound of Eric's voice that he loved telling the next part of the story.

"He stood on the dock with all of his clothes on. The boat came by and the spotter threw him the rope. I can still see it. I was always nervous, too. I think everyone was. We didn't want him to fall."

"He slipped on his skis without any effort at all, and then *bam*, with a roar of the boat's engine, he took off right from the dock. There was a huge splash and he kind of disappeared for a second. Everybody went silent until we were sure he'd made it. Then the place went crazy all over again.

"He was incredible. As soon as he'd planed off, he leaned down and took off one ski and put it over his shoulder. He was awesome — back and forth across the wake with one ski and one hand on the rope. He had a wicked big fantail behind him too. It looked as if he was leaning into the water dragging his shoulder.

"I guess the best part was when he came back in. He slipped his other ski back on as if it was nothing and then as the boat turned he whipped himself off. He was going so fast that he shot right up onto the shore and ran out of his skis onto the beach. Everyone went crazy, and he was barely wet above the knees."

So, explained Eric, Doug was the hero, and whenever any of the kids were having a tough time at camp, he got the call to help.

"We didn't know it then, but the whole thing was a plan. Doug asked Brian and me to help search out a spot on the lake for an overnight. We left in the speed boat after lunch on the third day of camp. By the time we came back about four hours later, neither of us was wanted to leave. We've been going to camp for the last six years."

"Do you see each other a lot during the year?"

"Absolutely. He's my best friend," said Eric automatically. "You'd like him. He's really crazy. He'll call up in the middle of the night and read me a couple of lines from some book. Then he hangs up without another word." He smiled and shook his head in disbelief.

The way Eric described Brian, he sounded exactly like Kevin. And as we continued to stretch, I thought about how hard it must have been for Eric to see his friend so sick. And then I wondered whether he was scared for himself, too. I didn't ask.

The first volley made everything disappear. I loved seeing Eric across the net. I felt stronger playing with him, for he knew. He really knew.

We laughed a lot and worked hard at the game that day. Neither of us talked about the tournament — that was something a lifetime away. For us, it was each stroke of the racket, each volley. For us, it was the playing.

– 25 –

It was as if I were going to a dance with the best-looking girl at St. John's. The blue shirt made me look too pale. The red one was better. And pants. I'd lost so much weight that nothing really fit that well. Jeans. Baggy or not, it didn't make that much difference.

I stood in front of the full-length mirror in the hallway looking at my Red Sox cap. I had to wear it; the thing was my trademark and good luck, too. Plus, I looked really sick without it.

The night before I had had a tough time sleeping – I was excited yet panicked about talking to Mrs. Brandeis' class. I actually practiced in front of the hallway mirror.

"I'm not afraid of dying." I spoke softly as if I had it totally together.

"I'm not afraid of dying." Now like a tough guy – kicking death in the face.

Too loud. "Got to speak softer," I whispered to myself. Firm but soft.

I toyed with other voices. One that sounded like a radio announcer's – too upbeat. Another that was solemn – too much like an undertaker's. I raised and lowered my voice as often as I changed my shirts that morning.

"Having cancer is like . . ."

I tugged at my shirt, tucked it in.

". . . like having cankers and hemorrhoids at the same time – it gets you coming and going – you can't win for losing."

Nah. I knew my father's old saying just wouldn't fit. A little too "flip" as my mother would say.

Flip? What the hell is flip, anyway? People flip off a diving board. Or you can flip someone off. There's Flip Wilson. The flip side.

You can flip out. Flip-flop. Flip your lid.

I laughed at the conversation I was having with myself. Nervous, plain and simple. But I loved talking to myself like that. I wondered if other people did the same. I couldn't imagine Mrs. Arsenault, the principal, talking to herself. Ha! Put her on the toilet talking to herself. Grunting away. I laughed out loud.

Who else?

Mr. Feltus, the 9000-pound driver education teacher at St. John's.

Holy. How could he ever maneuver himself onto one of those little toilet seats?

"Time to go," called my mother from the bottom of the stairs.

If anyone had ever heard what I was thinking.

"I'll be right there."

Mr. Feltus. I giggled quietly as I walked down the stairs.

Absolutely scared silly.

On the drive to Portland High School my mother struggled to find the right words. Finally, as always, she just said what she needed to say. "Are you sure you're ready for this?"

I looked at her closely, studied her face. I felt like making one of those flip remarks to break the tension. Something like "It's no big deal" or "I'll blow them away." But I didn't. I knew what she was feeling.

"I'll be okay," I said. "Don't worry."

But as I look back now, I'm sure she did. She knew how cruel kids could be. How thoughtless. And it wasn't that they really meant to hurt; it just happened. Like the time we were in the mall and a couple of kids started laughing and calling me skin head. I thought my mother was going to rip their faces off as she stormed up to them. Whatever she had said wiped the smiles off their faces in an instant, as if she'd driven her knee so deep into their groins that they wouldn't have been able to take another breath for a week.

As we drove, I had the feeling that she was preparing, sharpening her talons just in case.

Eric and his mother were in the main office with Mrs. Brandeis when we arrived. Once introductions were over, Eric and I drifted off together.

"Nervous?" he asked.

"I got the jitters."

"It'll be cool. You'll see."

"Hope so."

"Hey, if you can handle chemo and the fourth floor, you can handle a bunch of ninth graders."

We followed Mrs. Brandeis and our mothers down the empty hallway. I could hear the typical noises of school – laughter exploding from one class, test silence from another, and the lone monotone of a lecturing teacher spilling from yet another.

I stared at the walls and the rows of lockers as we walked. "How's Brian?" I finally asked.

"No improvement," said Eric. "They say he's not in any pain."

"I hope things go well."

"Thanks."

I felt good having asked.

As Mrs. Brandeis had explained, we would be speaking to four classes of ninth graders combined in a lecture hall. The room was large and brightly lit. It had off-white walls with racing stripes of green, blue, and orange shooting down the center. The chairs were blue and cushioned like in a cinema, and up front was a table with three chairs.

"We'll sit at the table," she explained as we walked down the aisle. "Eric, since you're an old hand at this, do you want to go first?"

"Sure."

"Scott, you just follow his lead," she said. "And don't worry."

A buzzer sounded.

Within seconds kids began filtering into the classroom. They looked like every-day kids to me. Some wore baseball caps, others had dresses on. They laughed and yapped to each other while Mrs. Brandeis walked among them. Finally, the late buzzer sounded and the place quieted.

I couldn't believe that Mrs. Brandeis didn't have to say anything to them.

"Good morning," she said.

"GOOD MORNING." The students responded in unison. A small

giggle rolled through the kids after the welcome.

"You sound well this morning," she said.

I watched and saw a ripple of smiles. I looked up back and saw Mrs. Burke and my mother; they looked comfortable with the first few moments.

"This is Eric Burke and this is Scott Cinader," she said pointing at each of us. "As I've told you, Eric has been battling cystic fibrosis for his entire life. And Scott has been afflicted with a form of cancer for the past five months." Mrs. Brandeis moved around the table that we were sitting behind and stepped a couple of rows deep into the audience. The students in the front rows turned around so they could watch her.

"Think about it," she said. "Think about what it would be like to be either of these boys." She turned and motioned toward us with her arm. "This thing we call life is very precious – I think you'll have an even better idea of how precious it is when you've had a chance to listen to these young men. Let's give them a warm welcome."

The kids clapped loudly. And when they stopped, Eric stood up and moved to the front of the table.

"Hi. I'm Eric Burke." He sat on the edge of the table and looked around the lecture hall. I couldn't believe how calm he sounded, how steady and in control he was.

"I'm a lot like you guys. I like junk food. I get off on music, and I love to dance. Sometimes I watch too much television. Sometimes I don't want to get up in the morning and go to school. My mother has to scream and yell at me to get me out of that bed."

The kids laughed.

"I dream all the time about stuff I want to do, and even though there's a chance my life won't be as long as yours, I still make plans and I still have dreams."

As he spoke, I felt my neck tightening and my mouth drying up . . . cotton-mouth, just like before a big basketball game. I didn't know whether I'd be able to get out one word.

"I don't want to stand up here and make a speech because that would be wicked boring, so if you want to ask some questions – any questions – go for it."

A nice looking girl with dark hair and dark eyes raised her hand immediately. "Mrs. B. talked to us about your disease, but I don't really understand it."

"That's a good place to start. People with CF produce stuff that clogs up their lungs and screws up their digestion. I won't go into all the medical stuff, but basically we get a lot of lung infections like pneumonia."

Another hand went up. "Do you think about it all the time?" asked another girl.

"A lot of people ask me that," he said, looking at me. "I don't really think about it all the time, but I know it's there. See, when you've had something like CF all of your life, you don't know anything else. You sort of just do what you do."

"But aren't you scared?" blurted out the girl.

Eric smiled. "No. Not really. It might be scary for you guys because death is a million miles away and because CF is strange to you. But as I said, I've lived with it all my life. Don't get me wrong, I do get scared and angry and sick of ending up in the hospital, but I don't think that I'm any different from you."

"What do you mean?" asked the girl.

"Well, don't you lie awake some nights and think about dying? About what it's going to be like? And don't you think about your folks dying, too? Doesn't everybody think about stuff like that?"

The girl nodded and so did a lot of other kids.

"I do. My friends without CF do. But when I'm in school and listening to my history teacher, I'm not thinking about cystic fibrosis. I'm not thinking that I might die next week or next month or whenever. I'd go nuts," he said throwing his arms into the air. "Most of the time, like in history class, I'm just trying to stay awake."

The kids broke up. Mrs. Brandeis smiled. Eric's magic was working.

"What about a cure?" asked a boy down front.

"I like to think about that. A lot of doctors and scientists are working on it and they're making incredible breakthroughs all the time. I'm betting on them."

"Me, too," said the dark-haired girl. And everyone clapped.

"So what about Scott?" asked the boy up front.

Eric looked over at me. Everyone did. I'm sure I looked scared to death.

"He's my tennis partner, you know. That's how we met," he said trying to give me a chance to stand up with him. But I didn't move. I froze. Couldn't get up. Couldn't open my mouth. Couldn't blink. I felt as if I were trying to breathe inside of a vacuum. My eyes began to water as I stared at all the faces.

Mrs. Brandeis was at my side in an instant. "This is your first time doing something like this, isn't it?"

I nodded.

"I'd never do it," said the dark-haired girl.

"Me neither," said the boy up front. "You guys have got more guts than I do."

A chorus of "Yeahs" sounded throughout the lecture hall.

"I thought this was going to be easy," I said softly, trying to clear my throat. "I actually planned all kinds of stuff to say. I even practiced in front of the mirror."

A cautious laugh sounded from the kids.

"I wanted to act cool, you know?"

The kids nodded, relieved that I was speaking. "I was going to say something like 'I'm not afraid of dying.' But that's not true. I am afraid. I'm scared."

Some of the kids leaned forward in their chairs as if they wanted to get closer to me. Mrs. Brandeis left my side. I stood up and sat next to Eric.

"The best thing is that everyone is behind me. My family. My friends. All of the doctors. It sounds crazy, but in a lot of ways I actually feel lucky." And without a thought I put my hand on Eric's shoulder.

He smiled, and together we tried to help them understand. Together, we shared our secret.

— 26 —

"Are you sure you don't mind my coming?" asked Lori as she stood at the front door of The Racket.

"No. It's cool. But you're not going to see very much. I can't play for more than twenty minutes most of the time — after that I kind of crawl around."

"I don't care. I just want to see you play."

Lori and I walked through the double glass doors. Eric stood at the main desk just beyond the entrance. He waved as we came in.

"That's Eric, isn't it?"

"That's my partner," I said as we moved toward him.

"Eric, this is my friend, Lori."

"Hi, Eric. Nice to meet you."

"It's really good to — "

"BOYS!" A voice bellowed out from behind the main desk. "I need to talk with you."

I recognized Joey Russell, the manager of The Racket, as he poked his head out of the office. I'd heard a bit about him from some of the guys — none of it was very good — but I'd never met him.

From what I'd heard, his father had made him manager, and the first thing Joey did was fix up the lounge. That made a lot of the players angry because some of the courts really needed big-time work. From what they said, Joey Russell didn't care, because he didn't play tennis.

"Come right in," he said, waving his arm. "Come right in."

Lori glanced at me as if to ask whether she should follow.

"This ought to be entertaining," said Eric. "You've got to come, too, Lori."

The three of us went around the main desk and headed toward a smiling Joey Russell. He shook all of our hands and pulled us into his office.

"Sit right down," he said as he moved behind his over-sized desk. "I understand that you two are going to play in the tournament?"

"Well," said Eric, "we're planning on it. Scott's a little wobbly right now, but he's getting stronger."

At first I thought that the man might be worried about some kind of liability. That he wouldn't want me playing because I might drop dead on the court. But Joey Russell had other plans.

"I think it's great," he said, smiling, leaning forward with his elbows on his desk.

He spoke quickly, reminding me of the used car salesmen on television. "You, too, can own this beauty!"

"Thing is, the way you two are . . ."

He stumbled a bit for his words, but didn't seem at all uncomfortable.

". . . you know, your problems, and being tennis partners. Well, it's great. People ought to hear about it."

"What do you mean 'hear about it'?" asked Eric.

"Ted Ryan is a good friend of mine. You know, the sports columnist for the Sunday paper?"

We all knew who Ted Ryan was. He had been a big-league baseball player until knee problems ended his career. After that he moved back to Maine to write. His Sunday columns were read by everybody, even those who didn't like sports.

"Anyway, he jumped at the chance to write about you two. Everyone would read about you. It's human interest stuff."

We looked at each other. I'd never thought about the two of us being interesting. Being a story people would actually read in a newspaper. I guess it made sense, but it felt weird.

"I'm going to waive your entry fees to the tournament and donate some of the tournament money to whatever you'd like."

"That's really nice of you," said Eric.

"Yeah," I added.

"Well, it's the least I can do," said Russell. "So where would you like the money to go?" he asked looking at Eric.

"For me, the Cystic Fibrosis Foundation of Maine."

Joey had his pen out and began to write. "Colistic? How do you spell that?"

"It's cystic, c-y-s-t-i-c, fibrosis, f-i-b-r-o-s-i-s." Eric spelled it out carefully.

"Got it," said Russell. "How about you Eric?"

"I'm Scott."

"Oh, yeah. So, where would you like a donation made?"

"I'm not really sure. Can I check and get back to you?"

"No problem. Okay, well, listen. Ted Ryan will be here on Thursday to interview you. Bring your smiles. They're taking pictures, too."

As we got up to leave, Joey Russell remained behind his desk. "Have a good practice," he said. "And good luck in the tournament."

"Thanks," we said in unison.

As I turned to close the door behind me, I looked back at Joey Russell. He had kicked his feet up onto his desk and wedged the phone up under his chin. Something in the way he looked behind his desk made me feel bad, almost dirty. But at the time I couldn't figure it out.

As we volleyed that afternoon with Lori watching off to the side, I had trouble concentrating. I kept seeing my picture on the sports page at one moment and then out on the court in the tournament trying to play three sets. I knew that that would not be a pretty sight.

After playing three easy games, we sat with Lori.

"It's weird, isn't it?" I asked.

"What?"

"It all sounds pretty good. You know, the money to charity and stuff. But something doesn't feel right."

"Well, there's no doubt the guy's a businessman, but as long as CF gets some money, I just don't care," said Eric.

"What do you think, Scott?" asked Lori.

"I can't last for three sets."

"Forget it, we'll put 'em away in two," said Eric, winking at me. "Anyway, who cares. All we can do is what we can do."

"That's right," said Lori. "The man gives me the creeps, but what the heck? You'll help raise some money and spread the word. It's a good cause."

At the end of practice Barbara Allen stopped by to chat with us. When we told her about the tournament and the article by Ted Ryan, she looked concerned.

"You need to know that I don't trust Joey Russell. When his father left, things changed a lot here."

"What do you mean?" I asked.

"His priorities. He spent a ton of money on that ridiculous wooden sign out in front of the lounge. He just doesn't think tennis." She grimaced as she spoke. "I'll tell you one thing, Joey Russell takes care of Joey Russell. If he's doing something charitable, he's part of the charity."

— 27 —

"They want you in for more chemotherapy a week from today."

"What!" My head snapped around and I glared at her. "I can tell you one thing, Mother. I'm not going into the hospital next Thursday. I'm playing in the tournament. I'll go in Saturday night, the second I walk off the court, but I'm not missing our match. I'm not letting Eric down." I spoke so quickly that I was out of breath. I grabbed onto the car seat waiting for my mother's attack. *A tennis tournament over chemotherapy.* I could just hear her, but I didn't care. I was playing — even if I could only handle one lousy set. I was playing. I wasn't going to let this happen. I didn't give a rat's ass about living or dying — all I cared about was stepping onto that court.

My mother didn't say a word. She never flinched. In fact, it looked like the corner of her lips were turned into a bit of a smile.

"Well?" I urged after a few silent moments. She looked at the road and kept driving. I figured she was using the old let-him-get-it-out-of-his-system routine. She was good at that; I'd rant and rave, and she'd just sit quietly until I'd gotten whatever it was out. My mother could wait better than anyone. She'd won more battles with me this way than I could remember, and after each go-around I swore that I'd figure out how to play. But I never did. I didn't have the patience. Like my father, I'd just lose it totally.

I turned and stared out the car window as the seconds of silence passed like hours. My mind jumped from Ted Ryan's interview to all of my friends like Kevin who were planning to come to the tournament. And without us at the tournament, Eric's charity would lose out on money. Not only that, a guy like Eric deserved some recognition.

Ready for a fight I turned and faced my mother.

It was a smile.

"Saturday night sounds fine to me," she said. "I'll call Dr. Schmidt."

* * *

"He'll be here in a half an hour or so," said Joey Russell. The sweat forming on his upper lip made him look sleazy.

"Okay," said Eric. "You know where to find us."

"He's different," I said as we walked away toward Court Eight.

"Takes all kinds," shrugged Eric. "Look at us."

"Yeah . . . look at us. The walking wounded."

We stepped to the back of Court Eight. Eric took out his Walkman and we sat near the back wall.

"Having second thoughts about playing?" he asked.

"Absolutely not. Hey, listen, I'm psyched. But I could use a hit of Chopin."

"Same here."

We lay back to stretch with the Walkman between us. Eric slipped his tape inside the machine and flicked it on. At first it was difficult to concentrate on either the music or the stretching. My mind drifted back and forth from the interview with Ted Ryan to the next round of treatments on the fourth floor. My stomach felt queasy as if I'd just flown over a knoll in a car at seventy miles an hour. I breathed deeply. Concentrated. Went with the music.

Neither of us heard the clicks of the camera nor the whispered, cautious conversation. Chopin had us once again. It wasn't until Jack Fredericks knelt down and touched my shoulder that I came back.

"Ted Ryan's here."

"Oh. Sorry." I pushed Eric on the shoulder. He opened his eyes by degrees and slowly sat up.

"I can't believe you got in here without Joey seeing you," said Barbara.

"Well, I ducked by the main desk when his back was turned," said the reporter looking over his shoulder.

Ted Ryan looked like a baseball player — square chin, wide shoulders, and sandy brown hair. He smiled and winked when he spoke about sneaking by the main desk, so I could tell that he didn't take anything, including himself, too seriously.

"I hope you two don't mind, but I took a photo of you while you were stretching and listening to the music," he said. "Is that a kind of meditation?"

I looked at Eric as if he should answer the question. But Eric looked right back at me.

"Sorry," said the reporter, "maybe I'm jumping into this a bit quickly. First of all, I'm not really what you'd call a close friend of Joey's if you haven't figured that out. We happened to be in the same fraternity together at college – that's all there is to that. And I don't chase ambulances for cheap, sensational stories. I write stories that need to be told."

Ms. Allen looked thoughtfully at Mr. Fredericks. I could tell she felt good about the reporter.

"And one more thing you might like to know," he said softly, lowering himself to the ground so that his eyes were at our level. "My mom died of cancer not too long ago. I don't totally understand what you are going through, but I have a feeling."

Suddenly, from the middle of the complex, a voice.

"Ted! Ted!" Joey Russell raced across the courts waving his arm wildly.

"Oh brother," groaned Ted. "Listen, why don't you guys play a little while I take care of the boss."

"Ted-deee," sang Joey as he stepped up to the man with his arms outstretched.

"Joe-eee," mimicked the reporter, shaking hands and skillfully avoiding the bear hug that Joey was attempting.

"Didn't see you come in. I was watching. Sorry about that. I was watching."

"Not a problem, Joey," said Ted graciously. "Let's let the boys warm up and we can talk."

Ted Ryan ushered Joey off the court while Eric and I prepared to volley.

"He's a smooth operator, isn't he?" asked Eric.

"He sure took care of Joe-eee, didn't he?"

Both of us laughed as we turned to watch the reporter, his arm wrapped around Joey, as he led him back into the office.

Our practice was sloppy. I could tell that both of us were thinking too much about the interview. Ted's question about meditation was on my mind; I wanted to come up with a good answer, but all I could think of was "Yes."

We stopped once for water.

"We don't have the best stuff today, do we?" asked Eric.

"Nope. I'm not with it," I admitted.

"It's hard to concentrate."

When Ted returned, Joey did not come with him. I figured he must have done some smooth talking to dump the guy.

"Are you sure that you don't want anymore time to practice?" asked Ted.

"No. Twenty minutes is about all I can handle right now," I admitted.

"Okay. So, I guess we should get going. First thing is, how did you two meet?" he asked as we all sat against the wall on Court Eight.

"We met right here. Barbara paired us up," explained Eric.

"So, who's better?" asked Ted.

"I've been playing longer," answered Eric immediately.

"He is." I jabbed my index finger toward my friend. "Definitely."

"I've played longer."

"Yeah. And you're better."

Ted laughed. "You guys sound like my brother and me. Well, except that we'd say it the other way around." He put down his long, thin notebook and looked right at me. "When did you find out about your cancer?"

"The end of October."

"And from what Jack has said, you've been through quite a bit of chemotherapy."

"Yup."

"Are you through?"

I hesitated. "No." Ted shifted uncomfortably. "I've got to go back in next Saturday."

"You didn't tell me that," said Eric quickly, turning his head.

"I just found out. Actually, they wanted me in next Thursday. Can you believe it? My mom's going to fix it so I don't have to go in until right after the tournament."

"You mean you're postponing your treatment to play?"

"Of course."

At first Ted was still – I couldn't read him. Half of me thought he was going to say that I was nuts and so were my parents.

"Why?" he finally asked.

I shrugged. "It's only a couple of days."

Ted smiled slightly and shook his head in disbelief. I got the feeling that he thought I was being really brave. I didn't know how to tell him that I wasn't. Part of me wished I could go into the hospital right that minute to get juiced so I wouldn't have to wait.

"How long will this series last?" he asked.

"About ten days, I think."

"It's tough, isn't it?" he asked.

"Chemo sucks. But as my folks say, I'm pretty lucky. Twenty years ago I would have been up a creek."

"That's a good way to look at it," he said, jotting in his notebook. "What about the music you listen to?"

"It's relaxing," said Eric.

"Yeah," I added. "It takes me out of it, you know? Out beyond."

"Far away," added Eric.

Ted scribbled in his notebook again. "What were you listening to?"

"Chopin," we said together and laughed.

"A prelude," I added as if I were a connoisseur of classical music.

I could see his lips moving as he wrote down "prelude." I couldn't believe how easy it was to talk with him. It was like talking to Kevin or Eric, not like some older people who took everything so seriously and who never cracked a smile. Ted Ryan was a regular kind of guy, and he listened.

"How does cystic fibrosis affect your tennis?"

"I'm not as big and strong as I should be," explained Eric.

"That's common among people with CF, right? Something to do

with digesting food properly."

"Yes, that's right. You've done your homework."

"And you take medication to help out with digestion?" Eric nodded. "And physical therapy, too."

"Yes, every morning for about a half an hour. It's called a percussion session. One of my parents pounds on my back and chest to help loosen the mucus," explained Eric.

"It's a lot to go through," said the reporter.

"Can't live without it."

Ted nodded thoughtfully. He paused for a moment. I could tell he was struggling with the next question.

"How do you deal with it?" he asked in a whisper.

Eric looked right into his eyes and asked, "Death?"

He nodded.

Eric and I looked at one another, ready to share our secret once again.

"We live day to day."

"Play tennis."

"Listen to music."

"Take our medicine."

"Spend time with our friends."

"And family."

"Sometimes I cry," I admitted.

"Me, too," said Eric.

"Really?" I asked.

Eric looked at me queerly. "Of course. What do you think?"

Ted laughed. Then, with a pensive look, asked, "Is there anything you'd like people to know?"

We both paused. For me, there were too many answers. Too many faces running around in my head.

Finally, Eric came through. "Maybe it's two things. One is that people don't have to be afraid around us. The second is that we don't need sympathy."

"Yeah. Exactly," I said.

Ted jotted in his notebook and then looked up with a smile. "So what makes you happiest?"

"My best friend, Kevin," I said quickly. "He's nuts. When my hair fell out, he shaved his head."

"No kidding?"

"Really. He's crazy."

"What about you, Eric? What makes you happy?"

"I know it sounds weird, but just about everything makes me happy."

The interview went on for over an hour. There were serious questions about breakthroughs in CF research and the chances for a cure. And not-so-serious questions about The Mosquito Test – Eric let it slip.

Near the end of our time together, it wasn't so much an interview anymore. We talked like three friends – nothing was off limits, certainly not the diseases.

As we were getting up to leave, Ted asked one more question.

"I know you guys aren't really the philosophical types, but tell me, what's life all about for you?"

Both of us paused and thought.

Finally, Eric cracked a small smile, and then we started just as automatically as if it had been planned.

"My family."

"Friends."

"The doctors and nurses."

"Tennis."

"Laughing."

"Crying."

"Him," said Eric pointing at me.

"Him, too," I said, jerking my thumb toward Eric.

"You guys are great."

"Well, maybe. But don't put any money on us for Saturday. We don't have a prayer," I said.

"I don't know about that," he said. "Seems to me you guys have something special going for you."

— 28 —

That Sunday the phone never stopped ringing. Friends and family called to rave about the article in the sports section. "Out Beyond, Far Away" by Ted Ryan began, "Last week I was given a lesson in life and living by two boys who play the game of tennis. It is a lesson I'll never forget."

"You're frigging famous!" shouted Kevin, screeching over the phone.

I could hear Kevin's mother scolding him in the background. "Don't scream! Your father's sleeping." Mr. Beane worked shifts at the local paper mill.

"I'm not famous," I said. "It's just a newspaper article." I tried to downplay the story even though I couldn't believe it had made the front page of the sports section with two huge pictures of Eric and me. One of the photos showed the two of us lying on the court listening to Chopin, and the other was in front of Joey Russell's sign.

"Everybody's going to read it. Everybody." Kevin was silent for a moment and then asked, "I'm really your best friend?" His voice was soft and meek.

"Of course. What do you think?"

"That's frigging incredible," he said.

"So are you."

"Hello."

"Hi. It's Lori."

I had recognized her voice.

"What a wonderful article," she said.

"He did a great job," I said. "But you know what? I feel kind of weird. Like everybody's going to be staring at me or something."

"Well, maybe they will stare, but I think it will be for all the right reasons," she answered. "I especially like this part of the article: 'Talking with Eric and Scott has made a difference in my life. Now, when the little things go wrong, I'll take a moment to think about these two boys, and how they live their lives.'"

"Hi, Scott. It's Barbara Allen." "Hi."

"I've read this article three times. It makes me feel good," she said.

"I liked it a lot, too."

"Scott, you're a very special young man, and I'm proud of you."

Shivers went up my spine as she spoke. I knew what I wanted to say in return and didn't know whether I could. But, it was almost automatic: "I want to thank you for everything. You're the best coach I've ever had, and you're one of the nicest people I know. You've taught me more than tennis."

"Thank you, Scott."

"Scott?"

"Yes."

"Scott, this is Don . . . from the fourth floor?"

"Hey, Don. How are you?"

"I'm awesome. I'm in remission."

"Great!"

"Yeah. I'm psyched. Hey, listen. I read the article about you and Eric. It's so cool. I used to play basketball, too. I can't right now, but I was thinking about tennis. Do you think I could come down with you guys sometime?"

"Absolutely."

"But I haven't played before."

"Who cares, Don," I laughed. "Don't worry about it. Now listen. I'm going in for another treatment, but Eric will be around. I'll talk to him and then give you a call."

"Awesome. Thanks, Scott."

"Hey, Scott. This is Vladie."

"How are you doing?"

"Great," he said lightly. "I read the article this morning. I know this is going to sound queer as hell, but I just wanted you to know how much it means to me that you and Eric are my friends."

"Hello?"

"Hi. Is this Scott?"

"Yes."

"Hi, Scott. It's Ted Ryan. I just wanted to make sure the article was okay."

"It's incredible. Everyone has been calling."

"I know what you mean. I've been getting a lot of calls, too."

"No kidding," I said. "I never thought anyone would call up a writer."

"It's one of the things about writing a column. People call," he said. "One of the calls I received was from my agent. She thinks your story would make a great book."

"A book?" I could barely say the word.

"Yes."

"You're kidding."

The man laughed. "I know it's kind of out of the blue, but I guarantee I'm not kidding. I've written several books for young adults as well as a couple of novels for older folks. Your story is interesting. You can tell from the response we've gotten from the article. I think people from around the country would like to hear about you and Eric."

I didn't speak.

"Hi, Mrs. Burke. This is Scott Cinader."

"Hi, Scott. A wonderful article, isn't it?"

"I couldn't believe it."

"Oh, I know. I can't wait for Eric to read it."

"He hasn't seen it yet?"

"No, he's been in the hospital all night with Brian and his parents."

"How's Brian doing?"

"His fight is over."

"Scott?"

"Yes."

"Scott, this is Mr. Russell."

Joey had a very formal tone to his voice.

"Hi."

"About the article, there's a mistake in the thing," he said. "The Racket can't donate all the money from the tournament to charity."

— 29 —

The parking lot at The Racket was packed with cars, but what really grabbed my attention were the two TV vans with radar dishes on top. They were from the local television stations, and there was no doubt why they were there.

In school on Monday lots of people said something to me about the article. Some of the kids even had me sign their copies, and they were dead serious, too. Mrs. Arsenault called me into her office to congratulate me; the ladies in the cafeteria were all smiles; even my biology teacher, Mr. Waite, said how pleased he was. But what was really incredible was the revised schedule of study on the chalk board. This time on the top of the list was Chapter twenty-three.

I asked my English teacher about Ted Ryan as a writer. Mr. Perkins said, "He's definitely up and coming. I like his style. He's bound to go places with his writing."

I heard Mr. Perkins' words over and over again in my head, and I pictured the cover of the book: Me and Eric standing at half court with our rackets. I kept wondering whether it would be a photograph or a drawing. Maybe pictures inside? All day Monday I was in fantasy overdrive.

Eric and I met by accident in the back of the parking lot of The Racket.

"How are you?" I asked.

"I'm okay."

"I'm sorry about Brian. I wish there were something I could say to you."

"The flowers were great. Thanks for sending them."

I had to admit it. "That was my mother's idea. At first I thought it was kind of weird to be sending you flowers. I was afraid you'd think it was stupid. But after talking it over with my parents, it felt right."

"It was cool," he said. "They came after I got back from Brian's memorial service."

My look must have been question enough.

"It's like a funeral, but there's no casket. Brian donated his body to science for research. We had a service at the college chapel; his father teaches there. Everyone came, and everyone brought something that reminded them of Brian."

"It sounds like the best."

"It was. We all had a chance to say something, too. I felt good after the service. It was as if I had been talking to him. That's what I want . . . I want my friends to feel good. I want it to be a celebration."

As he spoke, Eric's eyes filled with tears and his face looked sad and lonely. There was nothing I could say. I put my hands on his shoulders and then I hugged him. He sobbed and so did I.

After a few moments, we separated. I wiped the tears from my eyes while Eric shook his head and then ran his fingers through his hair.

"Let's get in there and play, partner." Eric swung his arm over my shoulder.

"Absolutely."

As we walked through the parking lot I knew from that moment on that Eric and I would always be friends.

When we stepped through the front doors into The Racket, the guy at the desk whisked us into Joey Russell's office. Joey himself was dealing with the press and wanted us to stay out of sight until he was finished. Figured.

The place was jammed. I could see the television lights focused in the midst of a large crowd. I knew that Joey was in the middle. I was surprised that he hadn't staged the interview in front of his new sign. He probably had been caught off guard.

"Crazy, isn't it?" I said as we walked around the office.

"Yeah. The thing that gets me is the book idea."

"When did Ted Ryan call you?"

"Sunday night," said Eric. "One thing is for sure, I'm going to play my own part in the movie."

"Movie!"

Eric laughed. "I'm kidding, Scott."

Right then Barbara and Jack stepped into the office.

"Well, the two stars," said Jack. His face was soft and kind looking. The hardness that he usually displayed on the courts had vanished. He looked like a different man.

"Unbelievable, isn't it?" said Eric.

"A lot of wonderful things have happened as a result of the article," said Barbara. "We've heard from over thirty families with kids who are ill or challenged."

"We're organizing a new program. Thinking about hiring more instructors. And Joey's talking about expanding."

"More courts?" asked Eric.

"Yes. Actually, the idea was his father's."

"But we'll let him believe that we think it's his idea," laughed Barbara.

"New courts," repeated Eric with a far away look on his face.

"There's even talk of a pool with a wheelchair entrance."

"All this because of a newspaper article," I said, shaking my head in disbelief.

"Unh-unh," mouthed Barbara. "All this because of two very special young men."

Jack chimed in. "Barbara is right. It's all because of you two."

The door opened and the guy at the desk poked his head in. "Joey would like you to come out and talk to the press."

"Notice that Joey didn't leave sight of the cameras for an instant." Barbara's snide tone was buffered with a smirk.

"Fame is fleeting. Someone like him has got to grab it when it's in sight," said Jack philosophically.

We walked tentatively into the crowd of reporters. When we settled next to Joey, the lights to the TV cameras snapped on. Once Joey introduced us, the questions came from everywhere.

"What did you think of Ted Ryan's article?" asked a woman from the television station.

I recognized her from the evening news. "I was kind of embarrassed at first," I said, squinting from the bright television lights.

"But all my friends in school were really good about it. They thought the article was cool."

"Same here," said Eric. "And I'd like to thank Ted. He did a great job explaining cystic fibrosis."

"Yeah, I want to thank him, too. He's a good writer and a great guy."

"Are you frightened?" asked a small woman who held a pad and pencil.

I looked at Eric. My mind raced. Everyone around us went still.

"About playing," she added quickly.

"No."

"As we always say, It ain't the Olympics," sparked Eric.

The woman smiled broadly as the rest of the crowd laughed. I could almost hear the sigh of relief.

"How do you think you'll do?"

We looked at each other and smirked. I glanced over at Barbara and Jack. Barbara rolled her eyes toward the ceiling.

Eric whispered into my ear. "Should we tell them the truth?"

I paused for a moment and then whispered back, "Nah."

"Well," said Eric, "we'd like to win."

"Do you feel a lot of pressure?" asked another.

"I don't feel any pressure about playing," said Eric, "but doing this is pretty uncomfortable." He motioned toward the cameras and the crowd.

Everyone laughed sympathetically.

"Do you feel as if you're playing for all the kids with cancer and cystic fibrosis?" asked another.

"I'm playing for him," I said pointing toward Eric. "He's my friend. I'm playing for my coaches, too. And I guess I'm playing for the fun of it."

"What he said," Eric added putting his hand on my shoulder.

"You both must be happy about the tournament money going toward research."

Eric looked toward Joey Russell.

"The Racket is proud to be able to help in the fight against these two horrible diseases. We're happy to donate all of the proceeds from the tournament to the cancer fund and to the cyst — ah — to Eric's charity."

I watched Eric's face crack into a wide grin. I thought he was going to burst out laughing. Some of the reporters stared at Joey in disbelief. He had almost pulled it off.

Court One had been reserved for us so that the news cameras and reporters could get a good look. As always we pulled out the Walkman and lay down in the corner of the court. This time, however, things were different. It was impossible to ignore the crowd of people who followed our every move, and I could actually feel the heat of the television lights. I closed my eyes and tried to concentrate, but it wasn't going to work. I knew I had to play along, so I faked it. I gave them what they wanted.

Later that night I called Eric.

"Did you watch the news?"

"No."

"You didn't?" I asked incredulously.

"Of course I did. You look weird on television."

"I know . . ."

"I can't believe how skinny I looked," he said.

Silence.

Finally. "It's kind of crazy, but I got a lot of calls tonight," said Eric. "Everyone's all hyped up about us winning."

"Same thing here."

"Worse than that, my father is the chairman of the Cystic Fibrosis Foundation in Maine. He said lots of people are calling to make donations. Some of them said they would double the contribution if we win on Saturday. Can you believe it?"

I felt as if I'd stepped into a fire. I couldn't take a breath, and for an instant I thought that I might drop the phone.

"Anyway, don't get any ideas," he said breaking the silence.

"What do you mean?"

"About winning."

"Why not?"

"You know those books you're always complaining about?"

"Yes."

"The kids in those stories always win something or do something really great that makes people happy."

"Yeah?"

"Well, then they die."

— 30 —

Ted took us out to dinner the night before the tournament.

"One of the problems we're having," said Eric, "is that a lot of people want us to win tomorrow."

"Some of them said they'd double their donations if we did," I added.

"Schmucks." Ted was disgusted. "I can't believe they would do such a thing. They're not thinking. They're just not thinking."

"We're going to play hard, but Scott's still not one hundred percent."

"Not even close. I wish I were. It would be great to play for real, and it'd be incredible to win."

"But," said Eric, "we're probably not going to."

"But winning isn't the point, is it?" Ted looked shocked. "I can't believe those people don't see that."

"They will tomorrow," said Eric.

"They'll figure it out."

The day of the tournament was spring-like. A warm breeze melted the last of the winter's snow, and the kids on the side of the road made dams out of mud and sticks. I remembered back to when I used to build dams with Kevin. Once, when we were about ten, we flooded the entire street in front of my house during a heavy April rain by plugging up a drain with plastic and building a huge dam. The police came and we spent the rest of the day hiding in the woods at our cabin convinced that we were going to jail. Those were the days.

The doubles matches would take place throughout the morning. Three rounds of single elimination. We were scheduled in the first round against a couple of guys from the Gorham Racket Club. Eric had never heard their names. However, we did know, thanks to some scouting by Jack Fredericks, that these guys were fairly new players but very athletic.

As we expected, The Racket was packed with people. The TV vans were back, too. The Burkes and my parents sat together just off Court One. Kevin and Lori along with a whole mess of teachers and kids from St. John's were lined up against the back wall. Behind them was a large sign: "Scott and Eric #1."

"That's cool," said Eric as he looked at the sign.

"It is."

"Look over there." Eric poked me in the arm and then pointed to the far end of the courts.

The sign read: "Fourth Floor Corps." I couldn't believe it. About ten kids in Red Sox caps stood with a half dozen nurses. They waved and cheered when they saw me staring. I lifted my racket into the air, and then, without thinking, I took off my Red Sox cap. They screamed even louder, and as if on command, all of the kids flipped off their hats exposing their lily-white scalps.

By now everyone in The Racket was watching and the place exploded. I turned and looked at Eric, but he was facing the other side of the courts. There, another group was going just as crazy as all of my friends from the fourth floor. I knew they were CF kids.

The two groups began chanting our names and the words resounded from one side of the building to the other.

"ERIC."

"SCOTT."

"ERIC."

"SCOTT."

In the midst of all of this, I caught sight of the two boys who must have been from Gorham. They walked slowly to their side of the court and immediately sat down to stretch. I could only imagine what was going through their minds.

Once the cheering quieted a bit, Joey Russell appeared.

"You guys ready?" he asked, beaming.

"All set," said Eric putting his warm-up jacket inside his bag.

"If you need a thing – anything – just let me know."

"Thanks."

"I'll be right over here." Joey pointed then stepped to the side of the court where I knew he'd remain for the rest of the match.

I looked at Eric. He had a slight grin on his face. "Let's stretch."

"Absolutely."

I had the feeling that I wouldn't be able to concentrate. The noise was worse than media day. Chopin was not touching me. All I could hear was my heart pounding, my whole body a gigantic thump.

"We could use some good old rock n' roll today," said Eric holding up the Walkman.

"No kidding."

We lay back and stretched. My mind raced. I tried to convince myself that I wasn't nervous, that I was focused on the match. It didn't do any good. I was shaking all over and needed to pee so bad that finally I jumped up and sprinted to the bathroom.

After I returned and settled down, Chopin broke through a bit. As I worked the muscles of my upper leg, I thought about going into the hospital that evening for my next series of chemo. Part of me was actually excited. This could be the end of it. Deep down inside I knew that I would be okay, that the medicine would make me well again. I knew that I was going to live.

At that moment I opened my eyes and glanced toward Eric. His face was relaxed. His lips were turned up into a slight smile – the look of satisfaction. I knew that he was loving every moment of this ordeal, of this torture.

I slowly scanned The Racket. I saw the faces of my family and friends. Looked at the kids like me and then the ones like Eric. In the far corner I could see Barbara and Jack standing side by side. And then I stared at all the faces of those people that I didn't know. The ones who looked at us with both fear and hope – and then the ones who never really looked at us at all.

The pounding in my chest disappeared with those faces, and as I turned my eyes back toward Eric, everything seemed to come into focus.

"Did he get you?" he asked, touching his earphones.

"Not this time," I said gently.

Eric looked at me and winked. Somehow I think he knew what was going through my mind.

The public address announcer spoke: "Would all doubles matches please begin within the next five minutes."

Eric put the Walkman back in his bag and we moved to center court to meet our opponents. The guys from Gorham were petrified. Their skin was pale and they fumbled with their rackets as they walked up to the net.

"They look sicker than we do," said Eric with a hint of concern in his voice.

I really felt sorry for them. They were in a no-win situation. If they did win, they would have just beaten a couple of sick kids. If they lost, they really lost.

"Hi, I'm Eric Burke."

"I'm Scott Cinader."

We both extended our hands.

"Ryan Murphy."

"Tyler James."

"Nice to meet you," said Eric. "Sorry about all of this hype," he said motioning over his shoulder toward the gallery.

I could see that these two weren't enjoying any of this.

"First tournament?" asked Eric, trying to loosen them up.

They nodded.

"Not exactly what you expected, huh?" I asked jokingly, rolling my eyes. "This is my first one, too."

"We read about you guys in the paper," said Tyler, his voice weak and cracking.

"Seems like everybody did," Eric said.

"I saw you on television." Ryan tugged at his shorts. "It must be cool – I mean . . ." His face went flat and his eyes widened as if he'd just been hit with a dose of the juice.

"We know what you mean," said Eric.

I thought the guy was going to lose it completely as he covered his face and mumbled.

"GOOD LUCK, YOU GUYS!" Someone screamed from the gallery.

"LET'S GO, ERIC. COME ON, SCOTT!"

The Gorham boys were in agony.

"Listen, you guys. Let's have some fun. This ain't the Olympics, you know," I said.

They smiled weakly.

"Come on, let's volley for a bit and get warmed up," said Eric. "Forget about all of this and let's just play."

They nodded, smiled, and wished us "Good luck."

"Relax." Eric shrugged.

"Enjoy," I added jutting my thumb into the air.

As we walked back to our side of the court, the crowd grew louder.

"I hope they can last the whole match," I said pointing back toward the two boys.

"No kidding."

Eric held a ball into the air and we began to volley. In just a few minutes I could tell that Ryan was about as good as I was, and that Tyler wasn't quite as steady as his partner. The big challenge for us was that both boys were very quick on their feet, and by their looks, they were in great shape, too. I knew that they could get to almost any ball on the court.

After a few minutes of easy play, we volleyed for service. The Gorham guys won.

The first game was absolutely pathetic. Ryan's serves were sloppy; he doubled faulted twice. I felt as if I'd never had a racket in my hand before. We played at deuce four times until Eric finally took over and hit two cross-court winners in a row.

The crowd went nuts. I saw Kevin and Lori hold up a bed sheet with our names emblazoned in red on it. One of the TV cameramen moved out onto the court to get a better shot of the crowd's reaction. All the time the two boys from Gorham huddled meekly at the back of the court.

"Nice shots," I said.

"Thanks. How you feeling?"

I looked right at Eric and smirked. I was winded and weak.

"That good, huh?"

"I probably have a set in me."

"Let's make it the best one ever."

When I served, the adrenaline pumped in and my body buzzed. The first ball hit the top of the net and fell back on our side. A groan sounded from the gallery. I didn't think twice after Eric retrieved the ball. I just served the sucker with everything I had.

That second ball went deep into the other court. Ryan barely got his racket on it and lobbed it harmlessly to the top of the net.

Eric's smash was a thing to behold. Fully outstretched, both feet off the ground, he drove it. I'd never seen a ball hit that hard before in my life, and I doubted whether the two guys from Gorham had either. We won my serve without much trouble.

Tyler was up next. He had a powerful stroke and great placement. Eric didn't have too much trouble handling him, but I just couldn't return his service. I simply wasn't quick enough.

The score was two games to one.

Eric's serves were monstrous. Neither of the Gorham players could catch up to them. The first was lined right to Tyler's feet. The boy barely got his racket down as the ball ricocheted off into the crowd. The next two serves were aces. Neither Gorham boy moved an inch. There was absolutely nothing they could do but admire Eric's power and accuracy.

When Eric finished off his service with an ace, the noise in The Racket frightened me. And more. Something within me started to say that we could actually win.

I walked to Eric's side and slapped his hand. "Great stuff."

"Thanks."

"We've got them on the run," I said.

"Yeah, for right now," he laughed, thinking I was joking.

At the moment I was serious, but I'd forgotten that I hadn't moved much during Eric's serves. He'd done all of the work, and I had had a chance to catch my breath. So when Ryan began serving, I came back to reality quickly.

Now, serving for a second time, the Gorham boy had calmed down. His serves were accurate and hard. We played long volleys which sent the crowd into frenzies and left me gasping for air. I stumbled once and then got a head rush.

At 30-30 I raised my hand toward the Gorham guys and walked over to get a towel. I couldn't take a deep breath and my legs were wobbling. My head began to clear as I toweled off, but I knew it was just a matter of time.

"How are you doing?" The concerned look on Eric's face made me weaker.

"Folding fast."

"Want to stop?"

I thought for a moment. "Not yet. Maybe I'll catch a second wind."

We played on. Fortunately, Ryan double-faulted when serving to me and then Eric struck a winner down the line on the weaker second serve. Somehow, we had survived and went up 4-1.

After a gulp of water, it was my turn to serve. My hands were numb and tingly. I was dizzy. As I stepped up to the baseline, I knew I didn't have the strength to serve the way I normally did. I couldn't get up on my toes. I held my racket just above my shoulder like a raw beginner and tossed the ball into the air.

It was pathetic.

The crowd hushed. They knew. My serves drifted weakly across the net. It took all of my concentration to make sure they landed in play. They were the kind of serves that anyone would have teed up and drilled for winners. But the Gorham boys didn't. They returned them as if we were volleying for the fun of it.

We won the first point. And then the second. Finally, I stepped to the baseline and waved Eric to my side.

"I know," he said.

And without another word we walked to the net and motioned for Tyler and Ryan.

"You guys are pretty cool to do what you're doing," said Eric, gently tapping Ryan on the shoulder with his racket.

"Yeah," I said, fighting the dizziness with slow, rhythmic breaths.

"But it's not fair to you." Eric touched Tyler on the shoulder, too.

"But – " Ryan couldn't find the words. Tyler looked toward the ground.

Finally, I began to see flickers of stars shrouded in a white film. I leaned against Eric and he quickly wrapped his arm around my waist.

"That's it," he said. "We've had enough." A bit of air whispered through my lips.

"How about playing this thing next summer?" asked Eric.

The Gorham boys nodded. Next summer it was.

— 31 —

Out Beyond, Far Away by Ted Ryan was published two years after the tournament. The book made the rounds of all the local bookstores but never really caught on big across the country. As one national reviewer wrote, "Ted Ryan's latest book is a sweet story of friendship and courage which illustrates his strengths as a writer. But in the final analysis, *Out Beyond* doesn't take the reader far away."

Ted's editor at the newspaper wrote an editorial response to the reviewer's comments. He invited the writer to "step out from behind your computer and take a walk in the real world." Sales of *Out Beyond, Far Away* doubled in Maine the week after the challenge was issued.

The book's overall lack of success didn't bother Eric or me; we were just too busy. The two of us went with Ted to a half dozen bookstores for signings and even appeared on the public broadcasting television station. I was amazed at how calm I was in front of the cameras. As for Eric, he was like an old pro.

The Racket did, indeed, sponsor more programs for the physically and mentally challenged. The new addition included four more tennis courts, two racquetball courts, and a complete exercise room. Barbara and Jack stayed on and eventually married. And as for Joey Russell, his father fired him when the Internal Revenue Service reported improprieties in Joey's personal tax filings. Barbara and Jack were immediately hired as managers.

Once I finished treatments for good and my hair grew back, Kevin let his grow as well — shoulder length. Everyone has been shocked by Kevin's success. He went off to college to study "whatever looks easiest" and came out a meteorologist. After a short and wacky stint at an FM radio station as its "weather guy," Kevin landed a position on television. He's incredibly funny and the talk of the state. The last word I heard was that Kevin's New York agent – yes, his agent – was negotiating a contract with one of the national networks. All this from a guy who snorted tomato seeds and downed glasses of chewed up peas. I wasn't surprised.

Eric and I did play the Gorham guys that next summer. There were no crowds or TV cameras this time, and we beat the pants off them in straight sets: 6-3, 6-2, 6-4. Afterwards, we all went out for pizza and talked tennis over five pitchers of root beer. I don't remember ever laughing so hard as we did when we talked about our first meeting at The Racket.

"I thought I was going to crap my pants when I saw those television cameras," admitted Ryan.

"I did," blurted Tyler, laughing so hard that a trickle of root beer dribbled from his nose.

Through high school Eric and I trained and worked at The Racket as instructors. We were always partners. We won our fair share of tournaments, but the best part of tennis was teaching the kids like us.

Together, we made scores of presentations in the schools and visited lots of hospitals. Just after we graduated from high school, we were invited to both national gatherings of the Cystic Fibrosis Foundation and the American Cancer Society. There, the two of us were awarded special achievement awards for our work with kids on and off the tennis courts. Eric accepted in the name of his friend Brian Colby. When I stood up to the microphone, I couldn't speak. I wanted to say how much I loved my partner and my friend, Eric Burke. The words never came. Even so, I am sure he knew.

— 32 —

In his last letter to me, Eric wrote, "It's the funniest thing. Last night out of the clear blue I started thinking about your club and its crazy initiation, The Mosquito Test. I told my roommate here all about it. We laughed so hard he almost ripped the stitches out of his side and I almost threw up. You guys must have looked pretty stupid sitting there in your underwear trying not to itch. I could never have done that. Never in a million years."

Eric died that next week. Like his friend, Brian, he had asked that his body be donated to a medical school and used for research.

I flew back from my job in California for the memorial service. Everyone was there. Lori. Barbara and Jack. Vladie. My parents. Ted Ryan. The Colbies. And perhaps best of all many of the kids that Eric and I had coached at The Racket.

Each of us brought something to share that day. Everyone had a special offering. Barbara and Jack told tennis stories. Ted read from his book. Vladie stood up and cried.

As for me, I asked a good friend to play one of Chopin's preludes. While she played, I stood at the podium and closed my eyes.

In a few moments the music took me away. I could hear all those sounds again — the solid *pop* of the ball, the screech of our sneakers tearing across the court, and the pounding of my heart. Then, amidst it all, I heard Eric's steady voice calling the score: "15 — love, Scott . . . 15 — serving — love."

About the Author

Richard Kent teaches English and directs The Writing Center at Mountain Valley High School in Rumford, Maine, where he has also coached soccer, skiing, track, and lacrosse. In 1993 Mr. Kent was honored as Maine Teacher of the Year. He received a National Educator Award from the Milken Family Foundation in 1994.

His previous works include a book of poetry entitled *Entering Weld* and a young adult novel, *Play On!*